M000211954

Rafael Sabatini, creator of so[...] was born in Italy in 1875 a[...] Switzerland. He eventually settled in England in 1892, by which time he was fluent in a total of five languages. He chose to write in English, claiming that 'all the best stories are written in English'.

His writing career was launched in the 1890s with a collection of short stories, and it was not until 1902 that his first novel was published. His fame, however, came with *Scaramouche*, the much-loved story of the French Revolution, which became an international bestseller. *Captain Blood* followed soon after, which resulted in a renewed enthusiasm for his earlier work.

For many years a prolific writer, he was forced to abandon writing in the 1940s through illness and he eventually died in 1950.

Sabatini is best-remembered for his heroic characters and high-spirited novels, many of which have been adapted into classic films, including *Scaramouche, Captain Blood* and *The Sea Hawk* starring Errol Flynn.

The Stalking-horse

Rafael Sabatini

This edition published in 2001 by House of Stratus, an imprint of Stratus Books Ltd., 21 Beeching Park, Kelly Bray, Cornwall, PL17 8QS, UK.

www.houseofstratus.com

Typeset, printed and bound by House of Stratus.

A catalogue record for this book is available from the British Library and the Library of Congress.

ISBN 07551-155-6-2

Contents

Contents (contd)

Chapter 1

Lady Lochmore

In this twentieth century the Earl of Lochmore would probably be described as a permanent adolescent. In his own more direct and less sophisticated age he was quite simply called a fool, and so dismissed by men of sense and sensibility.

There is little to be said in his favour. At forty years of age he was callow, obstinate, rather vicious, and imbued with more than an ordinary amount of the self-assertion in which a stupid man will endeavour to swaddle his stupidity.

You conceive that to the high-spirited daughter of that high-spirited chieftain, Macdonald of Invernaion, Lochmore was hardly the husband of her romantic dreams. But it was only after marriage that she discovered how far he failed to realize them.

In the brief season of his courtship she had perceived no more than the surface of the man.

And on the surface of him there was a certain deceptive glitter. He had travelled a good deal, and in his travels he had acquired a certain veneer, impressive to a child whose age was not half his own and who had been reared in the stern environment of Invernaion. For although her father's domain was wide – second only among the Macdonalds to that of Keppoch – and although he could bring a thousand claymores into the field, as, indeed, he had done at Killiecrankie, yet in the Castle of Invernaion life was uncouthly lived.

The pale reflection of southern graces in which Lochmore arrayed himself lent him almost an effulgence against such a background. His powerful, stocky figure, in itself inelegant, gathered a spurious elegance from his satin coat, his laces and silk stockings. His self-assertiveness she mistook for strength of character. Moreover she did not see it at its most flagrant in those days when his chief concern was to render himself pleasing. And so, notwithstanding the disparity in their ages, she had suffered herself without undue reluctance to be married to him, whereafter she had gone south with him to reap completest disillusion.

It was unfortunate for her that his qualities were such as to exclude him from the friendship of his peers. Men of birth and culture, the very men whose society he desired, were aloof with him. Because he found them so, he increased in self-assertiveness, and as a result found himself so shunned that to avoid isolation he was driven to low company. By nature crudely jealous, his jealousy was nourished into a singular malevolence by the fact that the persons of quality who found him repellent discovered attractions in his wife. Had it not been for her, his fine house in the Strand would have seen little of the company it was equipped to receive. As it was, this house became, in spite of him, a resort of men and women of that courtly society by which his lordship would have sought in vain to surround himself. But because in his heart he was not deceived, their presence brought him less satisfaction than secret resentment.

And there were jealousies of another, less general kind, resulting more or less directly out of this.

So recklessly, in his fundamental boorishness, did Lochmore manifest the bad relations which had come to prevail between himself and his wife, that more than one of those professors of gallantry who perceive their opportunity in marital discord, became of a particular assiduity in attentions to her ladyship.

Of these the most enterprising was Lady Lochmore's kinsman, the elegant, courtly Viscount Glenleven. He made use of his kinship so as to mask his approach, and assumed towards her ladyship a fraternal manner, which Lochmore, whilst observing it with suspicion, felt that he could not openly resent without rendering himself ridiculous. My Lord Glenleven, moreover, enjoyed a reputation as a swordsman considerable enough to be almost sinister. And this made men slow to affront him.

Slightly above the middle height, and of a figure which whilst slender gave signs of exceptional vigour, the young Viscount was possessed of a singularly pleasant, melodious voice, which had often served to correct the harsh impression made by his narrow face, with its hard blue eyes, long, straight nose and obstinate mouth. In age he was barely thirty and looked even younger as a result of the care he bestowed on his appearance. He was gifted, moreover, with a ready tongue, and could, when he cared to do so, display a peculiar charm of manner. He displayed it in full to her ladyship; but he displayed it in vain. Glenleven was an avowed Whig, enjoying a measure of favour at the court of the Dutch usurper; and this in a Macdonald was, from her ladyship's point of view, to be a renegade.

So utterly was her own romantic loyalty given to the exiled King James that she was incapable of understanding that any Macdonald should hold different sentiments; and since sooner or later the tongue must touch where the tooth aches, she gave vehement and downright expression one day, at last, to the contempt with which Glenleven's politics inspired her. She chose to do so in the presence of her husband, perhaps so that, obliquely, she might reprove him also for the complacency with which he accepted the usurpation.

Whilst Lochmore scowled and bit his fingernails, Glenleven smiled with a singularly sweet wistfulness.

"Dear Ailsa, there are times when it is possible to be right without being just. This is one of those rare occasions. Consider my shrunken means, so inadequate to my station. Active loyalty is a luxury beyond them. Our kinsmen in the Highlands may be as staunch as they please. They are safe in their fastnesses. But a Macdonald here in London must tread warily."

"A man may tread too warily for honour," said her downright ladyship.

This brought Lochmore into the discussion. "And a woman may talk too much for safety. My God, girl, have you never heard of treason and its consequences? Let me have no more of this Jacobite cant from you. Busy yourself with the concerns that are proper to a woman."

"You see," said Glenleven, with his gentle smile, "that I am not the only Scot who prizes prudence."

"Lochmore is not a Macdonald."

She spoke at once with pride of her race and scorn of those who were not of it. It was as if she said: "Lochmore is just a poor blind earthworm of whom nothing is to be expected."

His lordship, perfectly understanding, empurpled. "I thank God for't. You seem to think, girl, that all the virtues are resident in the offspring of that Highland dunghill. God a' mercy! Did you ever hear tell of the Campbells?"

"I seem to be hearing one now," said her fiery ladyship. "Only a vile son of Diarmid would speak as you do."

Here was a chance for the astute Glenleven; and he took it promptly, suddenly severe of manner.

"Indeed, Lochmore, you push insult a little far. You seem to forget that I, too, am a Macdonald."

"My wife's reproof to you is that you've forgotten it, yourself." With that jeer and a malevolent glance at her ladyship, Lochmore stamped boorishly out of the room without so much as a leave-taking.

Glenleven, standing over his seated kinswoman, sighed.

"Just now you uttered a veiled reproach of my prudence, Ailsa."

"I did not mean to veil it," said she.

"The more reason then why, if you need it, I should give you a proof of my courage." He touched his sword-hilt caressingly with his long delicate fingers. "Shall I prove it on that lowland boor? You have but to say the word, and I'll deliver you."

She sat quite still, with hands folded in her lap, a woman of an arresting beauty. Her neck and shoulders and finely chiselled face were of the warm pallor of ivory under a cloud of blackest hair above. Slender black eyebrows were level above liquid eyes so deeply blue as to seem black in any but the clearest daylight. The lips of her delicately sensitive mouth grew faintly scornful now as she considered his proposal.

"Let be," she said at last. "My deliverance is not your concern."

"If I were so to make it?" He was eager. "That oaf has said enough to justify me. I am a Macdonald, as I reminded him."

"And as I reminded you. He said so." Her scorn became more marked. "You are too good a Whig, Jamie, to have retained anything of the Macdonald but the name."

He hung his head. "Is that what stands between us, Ailsa?"

"It certainly stands between us."

"You know what I mean. Is that what prevents you loving me?"

"To be sure you have all else to command the passion."

"Why will you rally me, Ailsa? I am so earnest. So deeply sincere."

"But still so ignorant of what it means to be a Macdonald, though you profess yourself one. When were our women wantons, Jamie?"

"Love is not wantonness."

"So says gallantry. And the same of the betrayal of the marriage vows."

"Is Lochmore true to them?"

"We are not talking of Lochmore, but of you and me, Jamie."

"Yet Lochmore may not be left out. If he were what a husband – what your husband – should be, we should not be talking so at all."

She looked up at him, and her dark eyes smiled serenely. The habitual serenity and self-command of one reared in an environment that to Glenleven was nothing short of barbarous, had long been a source of amazement to him. Himself born and reared at a distance from those Highlands to which his family belonged, he knew nothing of that innate dignity and self-assurance with which those who sprang from its princely houses were naturally imbued. As reasonably might he have marvelled at those accepted marks of breeding displayed in her lofty countenance, in the proud carriage of her small head, in the fine shapeliness of her hands, and in her clean-limbed grace.

Slowly she shook her dark head. "This will not serve. You lose your time and destroy the little regard I retain for you. I do not love you, Jamie. Perhaps that is the reason. Anyway, let us leave it there, since that, at least, you must understand, whatever else may elude you."

"You do not love me," he said slowly, a touch of the tragic in his manner. "Is it because I am not a hare-brained Jacobite?"

"What a man! Does it matter why?"

"More than life. Show me the reason; and, if it lie in human power, I will amend it. If you cannot love me because you hate all Whigs, why then I'll cease to be a Whig tomorrow, whatever the cost."

"Vanity deludes you, Jamie. I do not love you because I do not love you, Whig or Tory."

He stood awhile silent, with bowed head. Then, since the heroic part was the only one which would permit him to retreat in good order, he played it bravely. He drew himself up, grave and calm.

"After all, to deserve your love was more than I should have ventured to hope. All that I ask is to be allowed to love you, who are of all women the most adorable. All that matters is that you should remember it against your need. If this boor to whom they have married you should strain your endurance beyond its strength, or if in anything else it should ever lie in my power to serve you, a word is all that I require. So that you remember that, Ailsa, I am, if not happy, at least resigned."

Chapter 2

Glencoe

Glenleven departed with confidence that for all her fortitude and respect for the marriage-tie, the day could not be far distant when Lochmore by his oafishness would destroy the one and the other.

And so, indeed, it might have fallen out but for a dark event in the distant Highlands at about that time, and its curious repercussion in the politically indifferent bosom of the Earl of Lochmore.

There were rumours in London that spring of an affair in the North, in which some Macdonalds had perished. But to London the Highlands were as remote as the American colonies, and there was as much, or as little, knowledge of and interest in their affairs. Even those whose acquaintance with Scottish matters was a little wider than that of the general, and who troubled to repeat the rumours, described the matter vaguely as an affray between Campbells and Macdonalds.

It was in vain that Lady Lochmore sought the detailed truth of these disquieting stories. Some accounted that the affair had its source in the eternal feud between the two clans concerned; others asserted that the source was political, a punishment upon some stiff-necked Jacobites who had refused to take the oath of allegiance and so profit by King William's offer of amnesty. But none could tell her what particular Macdonalds were involved. Few indeed among her

London friends could even understand what such a question meant.

In those uneasy days she leaned more than usual upon Glenleven, departing from the prudent coolness she had practised towards him ever since he had so boldly wooed her. The anxiety which she conceived that he must share, since he was of the same blood, set up a bond between them. In his anxiety to please her, Glenleven ransacked every likely quarter for news. But he could discover little. Trouble there had certainly been in the Highlands, and Macdonalds had been the sufferers by it; but what branch of that great clan was concerned could not be ascertained. The further one investigated, the more was one confused by the conflict of assertions. One day the tale would be that the Macdonalds of Keppoch had been the victims; on the next the Macdonalds of Glengarry would be named. Macdonald of Sleat was mentioned once, and once Macdonald of Invernaion. Not to add to her ladyship's distress Glenleven withheld this last rumour from his kinswoman.

Since her father had died at the end of the previous year, her brother Ian was now the head of the sept, and to Glenleven it seemed far from improbable that in whatever might have occurred Ian Macdonald should have been involved. He was of a wild, impulsive nature, as romantic and unpractical as his sister, and governed by two great passions: love of the House of Stuart and abhorrence of the House of Argyll. Consequently, thought Glenleven, who in all Scotland likelier than his cousin Ian to have refused the oath of allegiance to King William, and, thereby, to have provoked the vengeance of the Campbells?

And then, when conjecture could go no further, the whole truth was brought to Lady Lochmore by Ian Macdonald himself.

Attended by two grooms, who though breeched like Sassenachs, came bonneted and wrapped in their plaids, he rode in the dusk of an April evening into the courtyard of Lochmore's little mansion in the Strand.

The earl and his wife had dined, but were still at table when Ian, booted and spurred and dusty, strode into their presence.

Like his sister he was tall – a half-head taller than she – and like her he was black-haired and pallid, with the same dark-blue eyes and the same sensitive mouth.

"I come," he announced to Lochmore, "to beg shelter for the night. That and to embrace you, Ailsa. I am for France."

"For France?" the earl and his countess made echo together.

"To carry my sword to King James. To join the army that is mustering for the invasion of England. To lend a hand in sending this knavish Dutchman back to his cheese and his schnapps."

Lochmore was flung into a panic, for there was a servant present. "In God's name!" he cried.

The servant, however, was a Macdonald, who had followed her ladyship from Scotland. He had been staring at his chieftain goggle-eyed in incredulity. He was grinning broadly now at his chieftain's outspokenness. Nevertheless Lochmore was not reassured.

"I'll not have such words uttered in my house Ian. Are you mad? You're not in the Highlands now, where treason may be bawled to the winds."

Holding his sister to him with one encircling arm, Invernaion's face grew dark with scorn.

"Ye may be naught but a Lowland Scot, Lochmore; yet a Scot ye still are, and there'll be blood in your veins. Has it not curdled at what's happened yonder?"

"And where may yonder be?"

"Man!" Invernaion stared at him, and then at his sister. The blankness of her countenance, the question in her glance informed and amazed him. It was to her he spoke. "Is it possible ye've not heard what happened at Glencoe two months since?"

She shook her dark head. "There have been rumours, vague tales of an affray between Campbells and Macdonalds. But we do not even know what Macdonalds are concerned, and this although in my anxiety I have sought news everywhere. Nothing is known in London of the trouble."

Macdonald smiled without mirth. "It'll be known at Kensington, no doubt, whence the vile order came for that massacre. It failed to be as complete as was intended only because the scoundrel Campbells who did the Dutchman's bloody work happened to be blundering fools as well as cut-throats. But it's complete enough to cry to Heaven for vengeance. Not a hamlet, not a house has been left standing in Glencoe. There are some heaps of charred ruins there, as a monument to the false-hearted villainy of William of Orange. The Glen of Weeping has justified its name.

"You'll not say now, Lochmore, that I am to be dainty in picking my words when I speak of such a man?"

"You must be," his sister answered him. "Not for Dutch William's sake, but for your own, and for as long as you tread the soil where he is master."

"I give thanks that I shall not tread it long. Had it not been for the need to see you again and to tell you all, so that you may understand what moves me, I should have taken ship from Scotland."

He held her at arm's length, and looked with a fond, sad smile into eyes that were so like his own. "But it's a long tale and an ugly, lassie; and I am a weary, hungry man. And so are the lads who ride with me. Maybe ye'll give orders for their comfort."

Order for their comfort was given, and order was instantly taken for his own.

When, at last, refreshed with meat and wine, he sat back, it was to give them the full tale for which they waited. And it was a tale of horrors magnified by the treachery in which those horrors had been perpetrated.

He spoke as an eye-witness of the actual facts. For it had happened by an odd chance that on the 12th February he was on his way to the house of a friend on Loch Leven, to whose new-born child he was to stand godfather. He travelled accompanied, as now, by only a couple of his lads.

Delayed on the road by foul weather, they had reached the head of the defile of Glencoe as night was falling. And as it was a wild, stormy night of wind and blinding snow, he decided to call a halt and seek until morning the hospitality of the old chieftain Mac Ian.

Welcomed as a brother by that patriarchal Macdonald, he discovered that he was not that night the only guest. He was surprised to find two redcoat officers at Mac Ian's hospitable board, and none too pleased to discover a Campbell in the senior of these, Captain Campbell of Glenlyon.

It was explained to him that the captain and his lieutenant, a man named Lindsay, were in command of a company of a hundred and twenty redcoats of Argyll's Regiment, who for twelve days now had been quartered upon Macdonald hospitality in the glen. He had never quite understood by what pretence they had imposed themselves upon Mac Ian; but he had vaguely heard that they were marching against some of Glengarry's people who had been harrying the country. He had heard nothing of any such harrying, and the mere fact that these men were Campbells should have rendered them suspect. It may be, however, that any uneasiness Mac Ian might have felt was allayed by the fact that their captain's niece was married to the chieftain's younger son, Alexander Macdonald. The kinship thus established may, moreover, have been accounted to supply a reason why Glenlyon should quarter there himself and his men.

"That night," Invernaion continued, "after the two officers had departed to their quarters, which were at Inveriggan's, old Mac Ian and I sat long in talk over a bottle of old French brandy. He was in high spirits, relieved by the presence of these troops from anxieties that had been weighing upon him in connection with the manner in which he had taken the oath of allegiance. Never was bitterer deception, bitterer irony than that of his relief. You'll know the facts of the oath?"

They did not, and he, therefore, proceeded to relate them. Enthralled by his narrative, and the sense of tragedy which his tone and manner brought to it, they sat watching him with eyes that glittered in the candlelight.

"You'll know at least, maybe, that proclamation was made in Scotland of a general amnesty to all so-called rebels who should by the thirty-first of December last have sworn allegiance to the Dutchman.

11

"I know now that this was a trap in which the Campbell dog, Breadalbane, working through his knavish tool, the Master of Stair, hoped to take the Camerons and the Macdonalds. For it was added to the proclamation that after that date any who had not taken the oath would be pursued as enemies and traitors.

"Breadalbane's malice and covetousness built hopes upon our staunch loyalty to the rightful King. What he did not know was that we had represented to King James our inability to hold out, and that his majesty had intimated to us that he would not take it amiss that we should submit to the usurping dynasty provided that we held ourselves in readiness to rise against it when the time should come.

"So, one by one, we took the oath, until all save only Mac Ian had made that enforced profession of loyalty. Since our course was resolved, I don't know what delayed his submission. Maybe the postponement was prompted by repugnance, maybe merely by vanity to show himself more stiff-necked than his peers. We shall never know.

"Anyway, postpone he did until the last moment.

"On the thirty-first of December, accompanied by his principal vassals, old Mac Ian presented himself at Fort William to take the oath. To his dismay he was told that there was no one there competent to administer it. The nearest magistrate was at Inverary. In panic, as he told me, and cursing now a procrastination which might come to cost him his life and his estates, he made off in all haste for Inverary. But that is no light journey in the depths of winter. He was six days in performing it. Still, he carried a letter to the sheriff from the Governor of Fort William, which did bear witness to the fact that he had presented himself to take the oath on the thirty-first. The sheriff, although a Campbell, took a lenient view, administered the oath, and promised to send a letter of explanation to Edinburgh together with the certificates.

"Mac Ian returned home relieved, but in a relief that needed confirmation, for he knew the malice that was astir. This confirmation the old man thought that he possessed at last. This quartering of troops upon his people, he took to be a sign of the government's confidence in him; and it was stressed by the friendliness towards him and his of these troopers and their officers, who for twelve days now had been enjoying his bounteous hospitality."

He paused there a moment, his young face set and grim.

"I doubt," he said, slowly and sadly, "if in the history of the human race, with all the cruelty and the treachery that disgrace it, there is an instance of a blacker, fouler treachery than this. Compared with Glenlyon and the vile masters who sent him to the work, Judas, himself, becomes almost a saintly figure."

Then, with a sigh, he resumed his narrative.

"I was awakened, in the middle of the night as I thought, but actually, as I afterwards learnt, at five o'clock in the morning, by a shot in the room below.

"As I sat up in bed, listening, I caught distinctly above the howling of the wind, the sound of other shots in the open.

"With a sense of evil heavy upon me I jumped from the bed, hastily pulled on some garments, and with my plaid wrapped about me, went below. As I descended the stairs a woman's scream came to me from outside, then another shot, and a long wail that ended abruptly.

"I flung open the door of the main room below, and stood horror-stricken on the threshold. The chamber was in disorder. Chairs were overturned, and some shards of broken earthenware littered the floor. In a corner two redcoats were besetting a woman who defended herself feebly. It was Mac Ian's wife. Mac Ian himself lay, limp as a sack, prone across the table at which he and I had sat the night before; the table at which the officers had dined with us. He was dead; and just within the open doorway stood Lindsay still grasping the pistol with which he had shot him. Afterwards I was to learn that he had pistolled him even as Mac Ian was bidding him welcome to a morning draught, and calling his servants to come and minister to the soldier's needs.

"I was without weapons; but I advanced into the room.

" 'What is this?' I cried. 'What is happening here?'

"Lindsay stared at me. 'Invernaion!' he said, and laughed. 'Faith, I'd forgotten you. After all, you're a Macdonald, and our orders are that by daylight there shall not be one of that damned name left alive in Glencoe!'

"He called over his shoulder, and in prompt answer to it, three redcoats with firelocks emerged from the darkness into the lamplight.

" 'Here, my lads!' A wave of the ruffian's arm pointed me out to his men. 'Here's another of the damned brood.'

"That was all the command he gave them; all the command they needed; for they had those general orders that not a Macdonald, man, woman or bairn, was to live to see that day's light in Glencoe. They ranged themselves, and they were already raising their muskets.

"There was no reflection in what I did. Action anticipated thought. Before I even realized what I was doing, the room was in darkness. I had seized a chair that stood near me, and at a blow I had swept the lamp in fragments from the table. I leapt at the place where I had last seen the soldiers standing. The chair, used like a flail, met a yielding resistance, and I knew that one of them had gone down before me. I bounded through the gap left by his fall. Another bound, and I was in the open, where it was pitch dark and snowing hard. Curses followed me; then shots; then the blundering footsteps of those murderers.

"I turned to my right, whereabouts I knew of a ravine up which I proposed to make my way. I was not followed. In that darkness and with the hard-driven snow to render blindness absolute, the redcoats must have realized not merely the fruitlessness, but even the danger of pursuit.

"I stumbled upwards for perhaps a half-mile, and I came at last, bruised and with torn legs and hands, to a shallow cave, into which I was glad enough to creep for shelter from the pitiless weather. There at peep of day, I was joined by three other fugitives, one of whom was John Macdonald, Mac Ian's elder son.

"Glenlyon, you see, was a fool as well as a butcher. The plan of which he was given the execution, failed – God be thanked! – through his blundering. Had he kept to cold steel not a Macdonald would have escaped, and his orders would have been fulfilled to the letter. It was the shots that gave the alarm, and enabled three-fourths of the dwellers in the glen to take to the hills.

"The direct victims of that butchery numbered in men, women and children, something over thirty. But what may have been the total indirect number had not been ascertained when I departed. Scantily clad as most of them would be when they fled through the snow, many must have perished of exposure. Their lot is even more pitiful than that of the slaughtered.

"Late on the following day, by when the redcoats had departed, we crept down to the ruined glen. All that was to be seen of its prosperous hamlets were the smoking ruins of the houses the soldiers had fired. Nothing had they left behind them save the corpses on the dunghills. The whole glen had been laid waste; the cattle, sheep and goats had been herded away.

"A heap of ashes was all that remained of the domain of Glencoe, and the unfortunates who crept back, returned to find themselves without means of subsistence, face to face with famine."

He paused again wearily in that long narrative, paused as if overcome with the horror of it.

He poured himself a glass of claret, and slowly drank it under the sombre eyes of his silent audience before continuing. He spoke very quietly and slowly now.

"That evening in Glencoe I swore an oath upon the charred remains of old Mac Ian that I would take no rest nor thought for my own concerns until the authors of that abomination should have been brought to account; that I would spend myself without stint to accomplish this, and shrink from nothing that should forward that sacred task – sacred, indeed, to every man who bears the name of Macdonald.

"Of what I was constrained to suffer I will not speak. That is of no moment. I went to Edinburgh, there to ascertain precisely who might be responsible. And there, by cautious investigation, I gradually pieced the vile thing together, learnt of the parts played by Breadalbane and Stair. Their evil spite would not suffer them to receive the tardy oath of the Macdonalds of Glencoe. Enraged that so many whom they had hoped to enmesh in their pride and so ruin, should have escaped by stifling that pride, they vented all their evil fury upon the few whom a legal technicality left at their mercy. Vile as this was, viler still was the method adopted to execute their will, the treachery, the abuse of hospitality imposed upon their instruments, so that the massacre of the Macdonalds of Glencoe should be complete.

"But just as Breadalbane and Stair stand in responsibility above Glenlyon and Lindsay, so the usurper William stands above Breadalbane and Stair. For whilst either of these, or both jointly, conceived the order for the massacre, this William of Orange signed it. Oh, I know what I am saying, Lochmore. In Edinburgh my investigations were very complete. If things were not as I have said, if King William had not set his signature to that terrible order, justice could be moved against those malefactors.

"And so, the oath I swore not merely includes King William, but aims first of all at him as the master criminal in this."

Again he paused, and when next he spoke he had again reduced to a quiet note a voice into which vehemence had gradually crept.

"Listen, Lochmore, and you, too, Ailsa. This may surprise you. When I took my oath of allegiance to King William, I took it, as I believe that Lochiel took it, without any mental reservations. Lochiel announced the intention of coming to London to kiss his majesty's hands; and it was in my mind to do the like. All that is over now. In my eyes that have looked on the horrors of Glencoe, William of Orange is once more a usurper, to be removed from the throne of England by whatever means may present themselves.

"That is why I am on my way to France. And not merely to swell by one negligible sword the forces gathering to support King James. But to place myself unreservedly at his majesty's disposal, to be used in any way that he may account will help forward his restoration, as the necessary preliminary to retribution upon all those responsible in whatsoever degree for this odious crime against the Macdonalds."

He rose now, white-faced and fanatical of eye.

"For what you are, Lochmore, you owe thanks to his majesty's grandfather. What you have, came to you from his bounty. As a man of honour you will own the debt. As a man of honour I adjure you to seize every chance of repaying it."

Lochmore, from being deeply moved, deeply shocked by what he had heard, was now deeply startled. He grumbled dully that God was his witness that he owed little to King William or King William's friends. But this, he protested, did not help him to perceive what it might lie in his power to do.

Invernaion told him, and what Invernaion left unsaid was added by his sister, with a fervour even deeper than her brother's.

There was public opinion to be influenced, faltering loyalties to be sustained, slothful negligence to be put to shame. All this could be done here in London, and in this she was prepared – nay, eager – to do her part if Lochmore would either lead her or second her.

Thus for the first time in that full year of their unhappy marriage did a point of contact between them offer itself, did a matter present itself of which they could make a common interest, and so perhaps be yet drawn together, notwithstanding disparities. Instead, however, it was destined to lead to their final severance.

In the mention of what was to do, Lochmore perceived merely what his wife might do, influences which she might wield. For him there would be no such opportunities. Friendless as he perceived himself among her friends, he was not to be duped by her treasonable enthusiasm. He commanded none of the sympathy necessary to make his seditious proposals heeded. And from the resentful consideration of this and of his position among the Tories who were her principal courtiers, he passed to a no less resentful review of his position among the Whigs to whom he had so fruitlessly paid court.

He grew, perhaps, more deeply and sullenly conscious of his isolation than he had ever been before. He perceived the hopelessness of his case. Vaguely it was borne in upon him that at some point in his career he had moved in the wrong direction, and that his only chance of redemption lay now in an entirely fresh start. And just as he perceived this, so he perceived, too, that his brother-in-law offered him tonight the chance of making this fresh start in an arresting, even dazzling, manner. Let him range himself with Invernaion actively and militantly under the banner of King James; and when the King came to his own again Lochmore's would be a position of eminence, whence he could deal as cavalierly as he pleased with both Whig and Tory who had dealt so cavalierly with him. They should realize in bitterness the error of their sneers when they found him sneering down upon them in his turn, with a sneer that should have power to ostracize.

At least that is how Lady Lochmore more or less, and tentatively, explained afterwards to her brother the phenomenon of which they were now the witnesses, the sudden tempestuous impulse upon which Lochmore announced the unexpected intention of going to Saint Germains with his brother-in-law.

"It need not be publicly announced," he said. "Indeed, that would be rank folly. Ailsa will give it out that I have gone on the grand tour." And to this after a moment's thought he added with a little laugh of bitterness: "Considering what my relations with my dear wife are supposed to be, none will be incredulous, or even astonished."

Chapter 3

Invernaion

The mention of Glenleven by Invernaion, at breakfast on the following morning, came to give Lochmore pause in his impulsive resolve of the previous night.

It reminded him of all that to which his absence would leave his honour, in the person of her ladyship, exposed, and so reawakened the jealousy that had momentarily slumbered.

The Earl of Lochmore was of those who fail to perceive that a man who can do nothing to deserve his wife's affection, can do nothing to command his own married happiness, and, therefore, for his own sake, were better out of the chafing ties of that association. All that his lordship considered was that at law his countess was his property, and his jealous anxiety to protect her was precisely that which he would have brought to the protection of any other of his chattels.

This feeling, now fully aroused, might well have turned him from his purpose but for the connection in which Glenleven was mentioned. What Invernaion said was that the matter concerned Glenleven as closely as any other Macdonald, and that he should be informed so as to be given the opportunity of collaborating.

"Although he may have faltered in his adherence to King James, it will surprise me if when he hears the truth of this affair he will not be impatient to shake the dust of England from his shoes, and cross the Channel with us."

This made a difference to Lochmore. If Glenleven were to be of the party, he need not go back on his intentions and his word; there would no longer be the need to stay to defend his preserves from the one poacher he seriously feared.

Glenleven was sent for and came promptly. With horror and indignation he heard the true facts of Glencoe, as must any man who possessed a heart at all. In that horror and indignation he shed most of the Whig sympathies which out of expediency he had embraced. But he did not shed them quite all.

Not only was he a Macdonald of Invernaion, but he stood next to Ian in the succession to the chieftainship of the clan. It must seem to follow – and it certainly so seemed to the sluggish wits of Lochmore – that a matter so closely concerning Ian must as closely concern Glenleven.

What Glenleven's shrewd mind first saw was that directly the matter did not concern Ian at all. Vengeance was the business, in the first place, of the survivors of Glencoe, and, in the second place, of some of those Macdonalds who stood closer to Glencoe than did Invernaion. Ian Macdonald's assumption of the mantle of the avenger was fortuitous and emotional: a surrender to the passions aroused in him by what he had witnessed.

He moved Invernaion's indignant amazement by some such observation.

"Does it not concern every man who bears the name of Macdonald? It may move me more hotly because I saw with my own eyes what others have learnt merely from report. But to all Macdonalds alike it must be a clear duty to pull down the man of blood who ordered that infamy."

"You should not need it to be repeated to you, Jamie," said her ladyship in a voice of cold displeasure.

"I did not need it," he was quick to answer. For he coveted her favour above all things, and he instantly realized that for him to remain a Whig in the face of these events was to forfeit all chance of that favour forever. "You mistake me. I commented rather upon the oddness of the circumstances that this should fall on us. For I am with you, Ian, body and soul, brain and arm. It would have needed less than this to have aroused my duty to King James."

"Then you are really with us?" said her ladyship, melting a little from her coolness before this announcement of a sudden conversion.

"Could you doubt it?"

It was Invernaion who answered him.

"No," he said. "For then I must believe you at once without heart and without ambition. Your fortunes, Jamie, stand, I know, none so high. Here is the chance to mend them. It is those who range themselves at His Majesty's side now, in the hour of his need, who will sit beside him in the high places when he returns to his own."

There was a crooked smile on Glenleven's narrow face. "You believe in the gratitude of princes? Well, well! I, who do not, am in this for conscience' sake."

Her ladyship's glance approved him with sudden warmth.

He was brisk and eager. He would accompany them to Saint Germains. He would seek a place in the great army that was preparing to invade England, or he would serve in any capacity which might be discerned for him.

Thus was Lochmore's uneasiness set at rest.

When, however, Invernaion announced that he was for the Romney Marsh that very night, and that he would sail so soon as he could find a boat to put him across, Glenleven was not unnaturally checked. He could not, thus, at a moment's notice pack and quit. Some days would be necessary for the dispositions he would have to make. Either they must wait for him, or else leave him to follow in a few days' time, so soon as his arrangements could be completed. Besides, in those few days he might enlist others: men of substance and position in the country.

"It is not," he explained, "that these few swords can materially strengthen the invading army. But the men who bear them will be of inestimable support to the cause. Their example is one that will have many followers." He mentioned several titled Tories, such as the Earl of Claybourne and Viscount Preston, and insisted upon the effect upon the country of beholding such men in the ranks of the army to be landed. He mentioned even Russell and Marlborough, whom he knew for Jacobites at heart, and who might possibly be brought over definitely now.

Both Invernaion and Lochmore were impressed by his fervour and her ladyship's eyes sparkled at the prospect Glenleven's words unfolded.

"Woe me!" she cried. "That I may not wield a sword beside you; that I am but a woman."

Thus reminded of her womanhood and its troublesome contingencies, Lochmore swung back to his fears, and would have had them wait for Glenleven. But Invernaion would not hear of it. He was all impatience to be gone; and Lochmore, having now committed himself, could not withstand the heat and imperious will of his brother-in-law.

So that very day the twain set out for Sussex and the sea.

Her ladyship's parting kiss to her lord was perhaps the first kiss of real affection that had passed between them since their wedding. He was magnified in her eyes by the mission upon which he went. For the first time she saw him engaged in something that was not concerned with self-indulgence, something that commanded her respect.

To her brother she clung passionately for a moment, thrilled by an alarm for him which had been entirely absent from her embrace of her lord.

"God guard you, Ian," was her fervent whisper. "I shall pray for you, and I shall work for you here. You can depend upon me for that, and for all else. You have but to send me your commands."

He knew that he could so depend upon her. He had a high regard for her intelligence, and he was aware of the strength of her romantic attachment to the Stuart cause. He could desire no better agent in England.

Another agent, nevertheless, he was soon to possess in Glenleven. The Viscount gradually discovered that he had underrated the time necessary for those dispositions that were to be made, and particularly for the proselytizing work which he had announced that he would take in hand. Days grew to weeks, and still his departure was postponed. Finally, by the month of June, he found himself so deeply enmeshed in the business of stimulating active Jacobitism in England that he abandoned altogether – and entirely with Invernaion's concurrence – the notion of crossing to France. He could be far more valuable to King James at home, marshalling the friends of His Majesty, kindling loyalty in some and fanning into a blaze the smouldering embers of loyalty in others, by diligently spreading the true story of Glencoe. He would have, he announced, the nucleus of an army under his hand by the time His Majesty landed in England.

Ailsa Lochmore, observing his diligence, approved him, and, negligent of risks, turned her house into a meeting-place for the malcontents whom Glenleven was industriously assembling and stimulating.

Invernaion, informed of this in the course of the steady if discreet correspondence which he maintained in cipher with his sister, desired her to convey to Glenleven that His Majesty, sensible of the Viscount's diligence on his behalf, commanded him to remain at the post which he had created in London and to pursue the valuable work that he was performing there.

The only one who was not quite satisfied was Lochmore. He was pervaded – and probably not without reason – by a sense that he had been tricked, that Glenleven had never been sincere in the avowed intentions of following them to France. But there were compensations for him. He received civilities at the dour, priest-ridden court of Saint Germains such as had never yet fallen to his lot. He was happy in them because he failed to perceive that he owed them not to any merit discerned in himself, but to the fact that he was Invernaion's brother-in-law.

For Invernaion there had been the warmest welcome. There were too few Scots of eminence in the following of King James that he could afford to treat lightly the services offered by an influential young chieftain whose call would raise a thousand claymores in the day of battle, and who was, moreover, aflame with a holy ardour that would stop at nothing.

Such a man seemed almost sent by Heaven at such a moment. Louvois, that great statesman of Louis XIV, had devised the simplest of all schemes for definitely delivering his master from the anxieties caused him by the pestilential Prince of Orange. It was this William of Orange who held together the coalition that opposed the megalomania of Louis XIV, which would have rendered France the despot of Europe. Even to the genius of William of Orange such a task was not easy. Without him the coalition would fall to pieces, and its component members would lie severally at France's mercy. All that was necessary, then, to achieve this desirable end was William's removal, an entirely justifiable homicide in the eyes of Louvois.

Louvois, however, died before he could arrange for the execution of the scheme. But he bequeathed it, among other treasures, to his son, Barbesieux, who worked it out in detail.

The moment was propitious. William of Orange was in the Netherlands, at the head of the allied army, and at these headquarters would be fairly accessible.

King James was aware of and approved the simple expedient which was not merely to serve the ends of Louis XIV, but at the same time was to open wide, as he supposed, the door for his own return to his throne.

All that was lacking when Invernaion presented himself at Saint Germains was the instrument.

Now considering the risk to be run, indeed the practical certainty, whether successful or not, of being taken and of suffering the horrible fate of Ravaillac, an instrument was not easy to find. No brutal professional murderer or bravo for hire would serve. The task demanded some fanatical zealot on grounds be it of religion, be it of patriotism, who would be prepared to suffer martyrdom; and aspirants to martyrdom have not been common in any age.

Therefore the sudden but timely appearance at Saint Germains of this young Scot, his soul steeped in righteous abhorrence of William of Orange, aflame with the desire to avenge the blood of his kin so mercilessly and treacherously shed at Glencoe, appeared to King James to be a definite sign that Heaven favoured the enterprise.

"On my knees, sire, I beg you to let the task be mine."

A flame flickered in the eyes of the pallid, hatchet-faced monarch, who would, himself, gladly have gone on his knees to Invernaion to beg the service which Invernaion so fervently begged to be allowed to perform.

"Benedictus sis," he murmured, feeling that no lesser language than Latin was worthy of so sacred an occasion. "Accomplish this and rest forever in the certainty of my favour."

Invernaion smiled. "When it is accomplished, sire, I shall be beyond the reach of any favour but God's. I shall look to be remembered in your majesty's prayers."

King James glanced quickly down on him from the high chair in which he sat, a funereal figure, all in black save only for the bright blue ribbon of the Garter. He was about to speak, to rebut the assumption of such complete self-sacrifice. But the calm, smiling intrepidity of the handsome countenance into which he looked gave him pause. This was not one with whom it was necessary or desirable to prevaricate.

The cold, harsh face of the exiled monarch softened in its expression. For once perhaps that selfish marble heart was touched by pity that one so young and eager must be immolated in his sacred cause. But because his cause was sacred there could be no hesitations. He spoke softly.

"For those whose devotion makes for such sacrifice is the Kingdom of Heaven." Having added this to the Beatitudes, he fetched a sigh. "Go now, my friend. Tomorrow you shall have a letter from my Lord Marquis of Barbesieux, who will instruct you." He turned to his minister, Lord Melfort, who, behind his master's chair, was the only witness of the scene. "Go with him, Melfort. See him cared for."

Early on the morrow, however, before the King had written to Barbesieux there came from Barbesieux a letter by the hand of a French officer, named Grandval, which announced to James that the bearer was the instrument sought. He was sent to Saint Germains to receive His Majesty's benediction before setting out for Uden, whence he was to repair to the headquarters of the allies, where William of Orange was to be found.

The dull-witted King was in a quandary. He took counsel alone with Melfort. He was almost peevish.

"Voilà un embarras de richesses," he complained.

Melfort perceived no embarrassment. "A sign," he declared it. "A sign of the favour of Heaven, wearied, sire, by the iniquities of Your Majesty's heretical son-in-law."

The gloomy face of the monarch lighted a little. "It was to have been expected. Yes. I am a man of little faith when all is said, Melfort. But what is to be done? This Frenchman has already received his commission from Barbesieux, and I have promised mine to Macdonald of Invernaion."

"It is plain, sire. Should Grandval fail, you have Invernaion in reserve for another attempt. Should Invernaion go now and fail, you do not know that Grandval will again be available. That clearly indicates the solution."

Thus it was decided; and the French officer was brought back to the royal presence. James proffered his hand to the lips of Grandval. The letter had announced that the officer would have two associates in the enterprise.

"Go with God," James said to him. "If you and your companions do me this service you shall never want."

To Invernaion His Majesty was almost apologetic. But Invernaion's answer relieved the royal distress at disappointing the Scot of the crown of martyrdom. It was an answer that fully confirmed Melfort, and confirmed it almost in Melfort's own words.

"So that it is done, it matters little, sire, whose the hand. Should your present messenger have the mischance to fail, I still remain for this or any other service Your Majesty may command."

His Majesty was pleased with the answer, and thereafter Invernaion was honoured as an aspirant for martyrdom should be honoured by those on whose behalf he is to suffer it. The sun of the royal favour blazed upon him, and lesser mortals in the royal following courted and caressed him. On the other hand, it is eminently possible that jealousy was aroused against him for the favour shown him by a prince usually stingy in the matter. It is also certain that there were traitors at Saint Germains who kept the Government at home informed of what was happening at the court of the exiled king.

Be all that as it may, the fact is that when Grandval failed, betrayed by his coadjutors, and was taken, tried and executed, to the names of his associates published in England was added that of Ian Macdonald of Invernaion.

Thus for the first time did the name of that young Scottish chieftain leap into questionable fame in England. It was to be heard again a few months later, after Steinkirk had been fought and after King William had returned to England, when James Whitney, the highwayman, was caught and put upon his trial.

In an attempt to save his life, the ruffian announced himself privy to a plot to assassinate the King. Some eminent Jacobites had offered him, he swore, a great price to murder the King whilst he was hunting in Windsor Forest. He boldly named some great names, and amongst them was that of Ian Macdonald of Invernaion, who, he affirmed, had crossed from France to make him a specious proposal.

No credit was attached to his word, and no measures were taken against any of those he accused. But it was remembered, and was matter for comment, that Macdonald of Invernaion had been named also in connection with the Grandval attempt.

Chapter 4

The End of Lochmore

Macdonald of Invernaion was in close attendance upon King James. He accompanied him to La Hogue, and was with him there, waiting to embark for England with the army of invasion supplied by King Louis. There he witnessed the raid by the British fleet, under Russel, which destroyed at the very outset the hopes of that embarkation. He returned in the following of the dejected monarch to Saint Germains, sharing his dejection.

With Invernaion went Lochmore, shining in the glory which his brother-in-law reflected, and persuaded ever that he owed the favour in which he stood to the amiable parts discovered in himself by this discerning court. He was completely happy for perhaps the first time in his foolish life. He wrote vainglorious letters to his countess. So as to impress her with the consequence into which he was come at last, he packed these letters with accounts of what His Majesty had said to him upon this occasion or upon that, and with what answers he had dazzled Majesty in return. He gave the clear impression that Majesty hung upon his utterances.

At first his letters may have departed none too widely from the truth. But, little by little, his dull, contentious, unlovable nature coming to be perceived, men began to fall away from him here as all his life they had fallen away from him elsewhere. Because he could not brook this neglect, he met the growing indifference by an aggressive intrusiveness. Thus it follows that he made matters worse. He became the object of slights and sarcasms which, offending his vanity, stirred into full activity an evil, ugly temper, which had never required much stirring. It needed all the tact of Invernaion, supported by the respect in which he was held, to prevent an open rupture between his troublesome brother-in-law and one or another of the hotheads of whom there were plenty in the composition of that court.

In these efforts Invernaion was humanely seconded by a soldier of distinction, whose qualities had earned him a universal esteem at Saint Germains.

Colonel Dudley Walton had seen a great deal of French service, and had learned more than soldiering in the course of it. He was one of the very few who had the discernment, wit, and humanity to be sorry for Lochmore. He perceived the man's besetting trouble to be the loneliness to which he was doomed by the attributes inherent in him. Gross and coarse he might be. But underneath these qualities Colonel Walton caught glimpses of the man's passionate, pathetic desire for esteem and popularity such as he lacked the natural means to command. It was from this that his worst blundering resulted.

Colonel Walton befriended him when he was growing most friendless, and by his humour, tact, and skill kept the aggressive fellow safe for a season. But it was a wasted endeavour. Eventually the inevitable happened when Colonel Walton was not at hand to avert it.

The Earl of Lochmore occupied, as did so many other of the followers of King James, lodgings in the town of Saint Germains. These lodgings he shared with an Irishman named Burke. One night when his lordship had been drinking heavily he replied to a taunting jest of Burke's with a blow. From childhood he had been too ready with his hands.

A challenge followed.

Lochmore, in need of a friend to act for him, but afraid to meet the anger of his brother-in-law by telling him what had occurred, sought Colonel Walton.

The Colonel used every endeavour to compose the quarrel. He dealt with the two men separately; reasoned with each of them, more in the manner of a parson than of a soldier of fortune such as he was; and eventually he succeeded in bringing them to a peace-making meeting.

In this confrontation the Earl of Lochmore was his most sullen self, and Burke, a mere youngster, airily impudent. The Colonel delivered himself to them of a little homily upon the duty of keeping their lives at the disposal of their King who sorely needed them.

In age Colonel Walton stood between the two, a man in the early thirties, but in experience and worldly wisdom he was old enough to be the grandfather of either. And the calm suavity of his manner conveyed a sense of this. He was a tall man, straight, spare and vigorous, and of an exceptional elegance in all his appointments, from his black periwig to his Spanish shoes. His face was long, lean and olive-tinted, very square in the chin and firm in the mouth. His calm grey eyes were set at a downward slant, which lent the attractive countenance an air of gentle melancholy that served to increase its distinction.

If in all that court there was a man who commanded the gentle authority necessary to bring a couple of quarrelsome idiots to their senses, that man was Colonel Walton. But the present task was to prove beyond him. As he brought his little homily to a close, he seemed to direct his appeal more directly to Burke, or so Burke fancied.

He protested plaintively.

"Och now, hasn't there been a blow struck, Colonel darling? And would ye honour a man who could take a blow?"

"I would if he had provoked it," said the Colonel.

"It's the nice judge in a matter of honour ye are, to be sure, Colonel. And I'll take your judgment. If his lordship will apologize for the blow, I'll apologize for any provocation I may have given him."

"You hear, Lochmore," said Colonel Walton hopefully.

But Lochmore stood squarely planted on his thick legs, the very incarnation of obstinacy.

"I hear conditions," he grumbled. "Captain Burke called me a drunken heretic. I can take that from no man."

"Setting aside the matter of heresy, ye'll admit that ye were drunk," said Burke.

"I don't admit it, sir. I was not."

"Then more shame on ye for calling me a damned rapparee. I ask ye, Colonel, is that a thing a man can leave unanswered, now? If he insisted that he was sober when he said it, then it's devil an apology I'll accept from him at all."

"It's not been offered," snapped Lochmore. "If there are going to be apologies, you'll begin them."

"Not at all. If, as ye say, there are going to be apologies we'll have them in their proper order. Sure it's only to please the Colonel that I consent to this at all."

Colonel Walton intervened with a laugh, in the desperate endeavour to keep the matter light. "Come, come! Ye're both behaving like schoolboys. So that ye both apologize, what does it matter who begins it? Here!" He caught each by an arm, and pulled them forward. "Make it simultaneous by just shaking hands, and forget a folly done when ye were both the worse for liquor."

Burke let himself be drawn forward willingly. He was grinning his satisfaction of the compromise the Colonel had discovered. But Lochmore employed his weight to resist the Colonel's physical suasion. Observing this the volatile young Irishman, who had been ready to jettison all rancour, took sudden fire.

"Just look at the omadhaun's reluctance, Colonel. Sure it's the fight he wants, and, begad, that's an inclination I've never baulked in any man. To Hell with apologies." He wrenched his arm free of Colonel Walton's grasp. "I've none to offer now, first or last."

"I'm relieved," said his lordship. "I've never apologized to a man in my life."

The Colonel vented a sigh of despair. "I shouldn't make a boast of it, Lochmore."

"You are pleased to instruct me, Colonel Walton," said the quarrelsome fellow, climbing on to his dignity.

But the Colonel laughed, and clapped his shoulder. "Not I. Advice is not instruction."

"It is sometimes presumption."

The Colonel ceased to laugh.

"So it is. I'll presume no more."

The meeting took place next morning in the magnificent park of Saint Germains. On the way to it Lochmore, walking with a strut and a forward thrust of his incipient paunch, talked of what he would do to that damned Irish rapparee. The Colonel silent and dejected, regretting that he should have allowed himself to be drawn into an affair in which he could perceive only folly, let his lordship talk on uninterrupted.

Lochmore never came back from that morning walk under the dappled shade of those great elms that rose like the pillars of a cathedral to support the green roof above. The powerful, but heavy and sluggish earl, was no match for the light, quick Irishman, nor had he Burke's obvious experience in arms.

The fight was over almost as soon as it began, and Lochmore, his throat transfixed, lay on the turf and yielded up his foolish, obstinate, lonely soul.

Almost the only tears that were shed for him were those of Burke, who in an emotional storm of contrition called God and the Colonel to witness that he had never meant to do his lordship any mortal hurt.

Colonel Walton had a bad quarter of an hour with King James when he went, as was necessary, to render an account of the affair. Burke, on his advice, had gone off to report himself to Sarsfield, under whom he served, and to invoke that great soldier's protection. He was helped, too, by the testimony Colonel Walton gave of the young Irishman's willingness at one time to make the peace although he had received a blow. But Colonel Walton, who had enjoyed the King's confidence, bore now the brunt of the royal ill humour and left the presence with a sense of being in disgrace.

He sought Invernaion. Deeply shocked though he was by the event, Invernaion was not so shocked as not to be able to recognize Colonel Walton's good offices, however vainly employed. Warmly he expressed his gratitude to him for his endeavours and also for having stood by the unfortunate Lochmore in that disastrous meeting.

The only good that resulted from the deplorable affair was the bond which it set up between Invernaion and Colonel Walton, who became firm friends from that hour.

Chapter 5

Rejection

The news of the Earl of Lochmore's death was conveyed to his Countess by her kinsman, Glenleven, who, with great tact, came dressed in mourning for the occasion. Also he was aware that black became his slight supple figure and contrasted effectively with his fifty-guinea blond periwig.

He came prepared to offer consolation, but the young widow evinced no immediate overwhelming need of it. True, she went white and limp, and sat down abruptly under the shock of the tragic news. True, she shed a tear or two. But they were of a grief less passionate than had been Burke's. Her pity was chiefly concerned with the futility of her lord's end. Had he fallen in battle, or had his life otherwise been given to profit the cause, her sorrow would have been of a different order, full of reverence, and Lochmore's memory would have remained sacred to her. But he had died as he had lived, in no loftier cause than that of his blundering vanity and aggressiveness. Since he had never learnt, and never could have learnt, how to conduct his life, such a man was better at rest.

The news came at a time that was full of other preoccupations for one who was as stout and enterprising a champion as her ladyship of the exiled King. The disaster to the French Fleet that was to have convoyed the transports bringing over the army of invasion, and the brilliant affair of La Hogue had inflicted a cruel disappointment upon those Jacobites who, secretly armed, had been awaiting the signal for the insurrection. Despair had stilled their rising insolence. They made haste to bury their weapons and to hold their tongues. Further to repress them there had been some arrests, and these by a broadminded government that practised lenity as a matter of policy.

There remained, however, a gallant band which rejected pessimism, maintained a patient fortitude and kept its eyes confidently upon the future. Glenleven, so newly converted from his Whig sympathies had, after the fashion of converts, flung himself so passionately into Jacobitism that he was perhaps the most prominent in this band. His stout courage in that autumn of '92, his constant assertion that steadfastness of purpose must in the end prevail, was an inestimable source of strength to her ladyship. It enheartened her to persevere in spite of set-backs in the work of political sapping and mining which she had made her own.

Nor was it only on political grounds that she and Glenleven were associated. When the period of mourning retirement which the decencies dictated was at an end, she availed herself of the offices of her kinsman and was to be seen with him in public, at court, at the playhouse, in the park, and elsewhere.

Despite their close kinship Glenleven wooed her with a devotion obvious to all but herself. A man who hitherto had led something of a gay life, who was accounted, in fact, something of a rake, and classed by the puritanical with that elegant, accomplished profligate, Tom Wharton, he became suddenly a model of sobriety and circumspection in his habits, confined his gambling within harmless limits and forsook gallantry entirely.

Common report perceived calculation in this. But to the malice of the world of fashion that was inevitable. Because Glenleven's past bold play and general libertinism was known sorely to have reduced his never very considerable fortune, and because the beautiful and stately young widow was known to have been left handsomely endowed, it was assumed that his present circumspection was strategic. To confirm this it was erroneously assumed by some that Ian Macdonald's life was all that stood between his sister Ailsa and the possession of the broad acres of Invernaion. And Ian Macdonald's life did not promise to be a very long one, considering that already there was a price of two thousand pounds placed by the government upon information that would lead to his arrest.

They were not aware, those malevolent gossips, that Glenleven had wooed his kinswoman with the infinitely greater directness of an avowed ardour in Lochmore's lifetime, when there could have been no mercenary ends to serve. But then, had they known it, they would have said that this was no more than in harmony with habits which left the daughter, sister or wife of no friend immune from his pursuit. From the world's irresponsibly malicious tongues there is no security.

Nothing of all this, however, reached the ears of Glenleven. Again like that Tom Wharton, between whom and himself so many parallels were drawn, Glenleven could take care of himself too well sword in hand to make men careless of words uttered in his hearing. Serenely, then, he went his devoted, reformed ways, always at hand when her ladyship might need him, be it as escort, as counsellor, or as political confederate. In addition his presence did her the inestimable if unperceived service of holding aloof those other gallants who had been assiduous in her husband's lifetime, and, but for Glenleven, would have been more assiduous now.

At last, towards the end of the year, Glenleven opined that he had long enough practised reserve, and that the time had come to claim the reward of so much self-denying devotion.

He had supped with her ladyship on the eve of Christmas, and they had passed into the library, which was ever her favourite room. It was a spacious chamber, panelled in rich, dark walnut, in hue akin to that of the tooled calf bindings that along one side of it completely filled the shelves. For Lochmore's father had been possessed of an affectation of scholarship, and he had assembled and displayed here the outward signs of an inwardly absent grace of mind. His portrait by Lely, the only picture in the room, gazed down from its place above the overmantel, a dour, dark, puritanical visage, with the prominent nose and obstinate chin which his son had inherited. Tall windows, now concealed behind heavy velvet curtains of a golden brown, overlooked the garden and the water-gate, giving access to the river.

The room that night was at once warm and fragrant, from the cedar logs blazing on the wide hearth. These provided also, by her ladyship's wish, the only present light. It was snug and pleasant thus in that mellow chamber of which the leaping flames revealing much, left more in mysterious shadow. Its sheltering luxury was stressed by the moaning of the snow-laden wind outside.

Lady Lochmore in the depths of a winged armchair directly faced the blaze. Glenleven stood beside and a little behind her, leaning on the edge of the chair's tall back. The mellow setting and the mellow moment seemed to him appropriate. This, he felt, was his hour.

Bending over her, he broke, abruptly but softly, that spell of languorous silence.

"Ailsa, my dear! How long now has it been within your knowledge that I worship you?"

She did not stir, and from where he stood he could not see her face. But when presently she answered him, her tone held little promise of any responsive tenderness.

"I remember that you used to distress me with the avowal."

"At least, it need not distress you now. Now that you are free to listen."

"If you had waited until now to say it, I might listen less unwillingly."

"Can the torrent wait when the snows above are melting in the sun?"

"We are poetical."

"Why should we not be? It is the proper language of deep emotion, and – God knows – not inconsistent with deep sincerity."

She laughed a little, very softly. "How often has that sentence done duty already, Jamie? The melting snow, the torrent and the sun? How often have you rehearsed it?"

"Cruel! Why will you mock me?"

"It is not mockery to ask a plain question."

"If you so ask it, I must disdain to answer. I have said that I love you."

"You do not understand, Jamie. Had you not said it at a time when to say it approached insult… "

"Insult!" he cried out in horror, interrupting her.

"To an honest woman who has a husband, and who has made no sign to invite such an avowal, the assumption that it could be welcome is an assumption of her frailty. Is there no insult in that?"

He sighed. "Shall we leave the past?"

"It will not leave us, Jamie. It remains always, to be a part of the present. Had you not made love to me then, when to hope that I would listen was to hope that I was a wanton, I should hear you less mistrustfully now."

"You overstate that past," he complained, in distressed impatience. "You forget that you were a woman unhappily married."

"Oh, no, Jamie. I don't forget it. Nor that you were famed as a consoler of unhappy wives. You regarded them as your legitimate prey. No doubt you still do. We do not readily forsake our habits, and I should know little peace or happiness with a husband who had those."

"Ailsa, your words are killing me. Since I have known you, I have lived for you. No other woman has been in my dreams."

"Not in your dreams, perhaps. But dare you tell me how many there have been in your waking hours?"

He let his arms fall heavily to his sides in an expression of despair. "It is the eve of Christmas… " he was beginning, when again with laughter in her voice she cut him short.

"Oh, yes, I know. The season of goodwill." She rose, and turned fully to face him, a slim graceful silhouette against the firelight, her face provokingly in shadow. She held out her hands to him. "Let there be goodwill between us, Jamie. But no more talk of love, save such as should link two cousins. I have been married once, and God knows it was a dismal experience. Then I could not help myself. Now that I am free again I prize my freedom. I will never barter it except for the utter certainty of happiness. That certainty, Jamie, you do not offer me."

He had taken the hands she proffered, and he tightened now his grip of them.

"What can I do to prove you wrong?"

"Nothing, Jamie. For nothing would prevail against my knowledge of you."

"Ailsa!" His melodious voice trembled with emotion. The firelight flickering on his narrow face revealed in it an anguish of supplication. "Ailsa!" He sought to draw her to him, but she resisted, laughing ever a little in her determination not to allow the scene to assume too serious a note. Fearing to annoy her, he abandoned the attempt; but he still clung to her hands. He was very humble. "Ailsa, I understand. I see the prejudice against me. I have only the folly of my past to blame. But do not doom me to suffer all my life for that. Remember that a man needs inspiration to rise above the nature with which he is endowed. In you, my dear, I have found that inspiration, and since I found it my life has been ordered as you would have it. I will not press you now. But I want you to know that I shall continue so to order it. And this whether I am ultimately to win you or not. This because I cannot now hold myself. You are so much to me, my Ailsa, that I could not do otherwise."

The deep sincerity of his tone, and that musical moving voice, touched her senses if not her reason. Long afterwards she admitted that he had won with her in that moment an advantage which, if he had pressed it, might have broached the ramparts she had reared about herself. But his experience, although wide, did not run along these lines, and the sincerity that at last had entered into him made him falter.

She was so desirable as she stood before him there, so much a woman whose possession must fill a man with pride that he could take where she was concerned none of the gamester's risks, over which in the case of another he would never have hesitated.

Having spoken, he stood there, silent and still, like one who for the moment has no more to say. This silence endured some little time.

It became almost unnatural. Then, still without speaking, she gently disengaged her hands from his grasp, uttered a little sigh, and resumed her seat.

"Ring for light, Jamie," she said, in her even, friendly voice. "And bid Angus bring the punch."

Chapter 6

The Assassination Plot

Certain it is that the orderly circumspection of Glenleven's life continued very fully to be maintained, and that the town's worst tongue could find no grounds upon which to impute to him the slightest irregularity. His public reward for this was that the backbiters now sneeringly alluded to him as the reformed rake. His private reward lay in the fact that Lady Lochmore, hearing these sneers on one or two occasions, was moved by them to a greater kindness for him.

Apart from what concerned his hopes of ultimately winning her, their association in those days had become more close and constant than ever. Considering that its real source was Jacobitic, it was perhaps as well that in the eyes of court and town it should wear the veil of a tender motive.

As yet, however, there was nothing in their actions to draw upon themselves the eyes of a tolerant government. Lochmore House, it is true, had become a meeting-place for such avowed friends of King James as Lord Claybourne, Sir Hamish Stuart of Meorach, Major Denis O'Grady, Sir John Fenwick and that Sir John Friend who so lavishly spent on sedition the great fortune he had amassed from brewing. But so long as they came there to discuss the long-drawn war with France and the grievances to which it was giving rise, the abject state of the currency and the ever-increasing confusion

41

resulting from it; to express the faith born of hope that soon the entire country, weary of the usurper's misgovernment, would be ready to rise and to drink to the health of the King over the Water; so long they attracted no attention. Nor for some time did they, nor, for that matter, did any other of the numerous groups of Jacobites astir in the country, do more than talk.

Not until the comparatively sudden death of the gentle and amiable Queen Mary did the season for activity appear to have arrived.

Whilst the interminable war dragged on, it was necessary for King William to spend half the year in camp, out of England. Hitherto in his absences the ship of state had been steered safely and shrewdly by the Queen. Who, it was asked, would steer it now?

The position of this Dutchman who governed England, always precarious, appeared all at once to have become impossible. And King William, crushed under the burden of his sorrow at the loss of one so truly dear to him, seemed by the numbness of his spirit to improve the opportunity of his enemies.

No time was lost in seizing it.

Suddenly, unheralded, reckless of the price upon his head, Invernaion arrived in London. He came straight to his sister's house, which he knew would offer him a safe asylum; for nowadays she employed no single servant, male or female, who was not a Macdonald. For the same reason he announced to her, as soon as a fond greeting, spiced on her side by a tender alarm, had passed between them, and when she came to question him upon the motives of his presence, that he had given appointment there to two loyal friends of King James who were to co-operate with him in what he came to do.

The gladness of her welcome to him was quickened rather than diminished by his news, all eager and zealous as she was to serve the cause of the rightful King.

That these two loyal friends of exiled Majesty when on the morrow they punctually presented themselves, were anything but prepossessing nowise reduced her enthusiasm.

The first of them was Robert Charnock, a pompous, middle-aged gentleman, unctuous of manner and booming of voice, who had been Vice-President of Magdalen College, Oxford, in the late reign. The other was George Porter, a slim, saturnine man of easy manners, who assumed almost from the outset an attitude of gallantry towards her ladyship. He was accompanied by a Frenchman, named de la Rue, a raffish fellow, who enjoyed a certain unsavoury reputation as a gambler, and bully, and who, even more outrageously than his sponsor, glowed and smirked and peacocked before his hostess.

They were, it will be seen, plotters of a very different type from the courtly dilettanti in treason whom her ladyship was in the habit of entertaining at her seditious gatherings. Nevertheless, for the sake of what her brother had told her that they were prepared to do for the cause, she made them welcome and steeled herself to endure them.

Glenleven, Fenwick and Friend, who had been hastily summoned, were also present; and they served to supply a certain leaven of decency to the gathering. Assembled in the library, that group of conspirators heard from Invernaion what it was that he had crossed the Channel to propose.

It was a simple plot, in all but the execution. Now that Queen Mary was dead and buried, the sudden removal of the usurper before he could appoint a regent to represent him in his absences must result in chaos. Of this that vast majority of Englishmen who were faithful to King James could not fail to take advantage.

The aim, then – and Ian Macdonald displayed to them his commission from the exiled King – was to seize the person of William of Orange. He was to be carried to France, where King Louis would find a lodging for him whence he would never again emerge to disturb the world.

Invernaion explained that Charnock and Porter had been indicated to him as resolute, enterprising men, who would know how to assist him in the execution of this design, and he invited not only these but also the others present to put forward suggestions of ways and means by which the kidnapping might best be accomplished.

Porter promptly gave the enterprise his benediction, and swaggeringly announced himself at the orders of Invernaion. Charnock, with less swagger, went further. He professed an eagerness himself to plot the details when he should have considered exactly the time and place most suitable, and he expressed a solid confidence in his ability to do so with advantage. Also he boasted himself prepared and able to find the considerable body of men which would be necessary for the execution of a scheme at once so bold and so difficult.

De la Rue, in a sense, went further still.

"I ask myself – nom de Dieu! – what for all this plaguey trouble of kidnapping him, when a bullet will do the affair so much more simply."

Porter, equally bloodthirsty, gave the Frenchman his prompt support.

"In God's name, why not? It's cleaner and quicker, and it will need fewer hands. Therefore the risk will be less."

Invernaion's grave dark eyes looked from one to the other of them.

"For my own part, I have no arguments to oppose to you, save that killing is not in my orders. These are definite. So, by your leave, sirs, we will keep to them."

"I am relieved to hear it," put in Sir John Fenwick. "For I tell you roundly that murder is not at all to my taste."

Sir John Friend solemnly nodded his support of Fenwick. "Myself, I could even wish that your orders did not go as far as they do. I am ready to spend my last crown in promoting a rising and in mounting and equipping men, but I have little stomach for schemes of violence against one man."

Glenleven's melodious voice interposed.

"We should hardly allow squeamishness to dictate our course in dealing with one who, himself, has never shrunk from violence. Even if murder were the proposal, I, for one, should remember that we would be paying the murderer of Glencoe in his own coin."

"That," said Invernaion, "was my own argument at Saint Germains. But I was overborne."

"Thank God you were," said Friend, with fervour. "For it was an argument upon a false premise. The news may not have reached you in France, sir, that the business of Glencoe has lately been the subject of a commission of inquiry."

He addressed himself to Invernaion, but it was Glenleven who answered him.

"Whether Invernaion has heard of it or not, I have certainly heard of it. You will conceive my interest. But you will not fail to weigh, Sir John, that the commission pronounced the affair an act of murder."

The portly little man swung to him, with some heat. He was emphatic. "But not against King William," he declared. "It came out in the inquiry that the order signed by him could not be construed as a warrant for the butchery that was perpetrated."

"Then why," asked Glenleven, "are not those prosecuted who maliciously so construed it?"

"You know that they are," Fenwick intervened. "Hamilton, Glenlyon, and Lindsay will be hanged when taken."

"And the Master of Stair?" asked her ladyship in a cold, hard voice. "And Breadalbane?"

Fenwick looked at her in surprise, and read in her pinched lips and pallid cheeks the depth of emotion stirring in her.

"The Master of Stair," he gently reminded her, "has been disgraced by the King."

She laughed without mirth. "That contents you, Sir John? The officers who executed the explicit orders of the Master of Stair are being hunted as murderers. But the man who issued the order, the huntsman who unleashed those dogs upon the quarry, is merely disgraced. Does that look as if he has misconstrued the order he received in his turn from above? Is not the conclusion that those poor tools of his who are being pursued for murder, are mere scapegoats, sacrifices offered up to the indignation that has been aroused in every humane heart?"

Sir John was continuing to stare at her, surprised at once by her vehemence and her lucidity. Invernaion, who had been silently attentive, explained her.

"We are Macdonalds, Sir John: my sister and I. To us this is a family affair. The blood so remorselessly shed was the blood of our kin."

Fenwick bowed his fine head in understanding. Not so, however, Sir John Friend. He took up the argument. "Do not, I beg you, allow that circumstance to obscure your judgment, as it so easily may. Where is King William's motive for ordering that massacre? What possible object could he hope to serve? Can you suppose that this Dutchman, who has never even been in Scotland, could have been concerned to order a slaughter of Macdonalds. Isn't it plain that it was he who was a tool? That he was misled by those of his advisers who had a grudge against the men of your clan?"

"It might be plain," said Invernaion, "if he had hanged Stair and Breadalbane."

And again her ladyship laughed, this time at the readiness of her brother's retort. She leaned across the table about which they were grouped. "Ay! Answer that, Sir John," she challenged the brewer-knight.

"It is easily answered, my lady," he was beginning, when Charnock, out of patience, interrupted him in his booming voice.

"My dear Sir John, I begin to suspect that you are well-named Friend. King William's friend."

De la Rue smacked the dust out of his breeches to the accompaniment of a horse-laugh at the gibe. Porter grinned broadly, whilst the others gravely considered the little brewer's spluttering confusion.

"You are me-merry, sir," he protested. "None knows be-better than yourself how far that is untrue. I'm a non-juror, as all the world knows. Just as all the world knows that Sir John Fenwick, there, who is laughing at me, took the oath."

Fenwick, a passionate man, flushed darkly. "It looks as if we might both be liars, then."

This brought Friend in anger to his feet. "I take that ill, Sir John." By the look of him he would have added a good deal more had not her ladyship rapped the table with her knuckles and called them both to order.

"Are you not wasting time and tempers, sirs? It is a way of your sex to reproach mine with inconclusive wordiness. But whither are you straying now?"

Fenwick was instantly submissive. He bowed his head to her until his face was in the shadow of his periwig. "We deserve the rebuke. Do we not, Sir John?"

Friend gave a grumbling agreement, and then begged to be allowed to take his leave. King James, he protested, had no more loyal subject than himself. For what concerned a rising, the provision of arms, the equipping and mounting of men, and the like, they could call upon him to disburse his last shilling. But since his conscience was opposed to any other ways of over-setting the throne, there could be no profit to themselves or to him in his remaining now.

He was allowed to go, and his departure became the signal for the breaking-up of that meeting, since nothing further was to be done by talking until ways and means had been devised, or, at least, until some practical suggestion could be tabled. Charnock and his associates were to communicate with Invernaion again as soon as they should have a settled plan to lay before him.

But although there were further meetings in the days that followed, and in spite of Charnock's confidence in his invention, of practical suggestions there were none. And this because it was realized by all of them when they came to grips with the question that the difficulties of kidnapping King William were almost insuperable.

Once these difficulties were recognized by Invernaion, Charnock put forward, indeed, a plan. But it was simply a plan of assassination.

As before, Invernaion acknowledged that he did not shrink from such an act, but reminded them again that his hands were tied by his commission, which did not permit him to authorize murder.

In this deadlock he was urged by Charnock and Porter to return to Saint Germains, to expound there the situation as he now understood it, and to endeavour to prevail upon King James to widen the scope of the commission.

So back to France went Invernaion, whilst the conspirators in London held themselves in readiness against his return, and in the meantime were busy recruiting further Jacobites to the enterprise.

But weeks passed without Invernaion's reappearance, the reason being that at Saint Germains and Versailles wider measures were being concerted than at first had been contemplated, and time was necessary for these.

Finally, the spring being well advanced, King William sailed for the Netherlands to resume the campaign, thus rendering impossible the execution of any plot against his person until his army should once more have gone into winter quarters.

But by the time he came back in the autumn, increased in credit by his victory at Namur, not only was everything ready, but King James, himself, was now a very active participant in what was to do. The Duke of Berwick was secretly in England, accompanied by Colonel Walton, to organize a Jacobite rising in strength. King James was on his way to Calais to place himself at the head of twelve thousand French troops lent to him by Louis XIV, with which to come to the support of his loyal subjects so soon as the rising took place.

The moment for this rising should be that of the confusion resulting from the death of William of Orange, a death which consequently was now an integral part of the great plan.

To direct this initial step, Invernaion returned at last, accompanied by Sir George Barclay, who seems in many ways to have been employed as a mask for him. This time Ian Macdonald came fortified by a commission from King James widened to the point of authorizing him to "undertake against the Prince of Orange such acts of hostility as should most conduce to the service of the King."

A few specially selected officers followed, and these and others who desired to communicate with the royal agent were informed that he was to be found on Mondays and Thursdays after nightfall walking in the Piazza at Covent Garden with a white handkerchief hanging from his pocket.

This agent was sometimes Ian Macdonald himself, but more commonly Sir George Barclay, who would pass on these applicants and recruits to Invernaion.

Invernaion meanwhile had resumed communication with those leaders, Charnock, Porter, de la Rue, and yet another named Cardell Goodman, and through them he made the acquaintance of many more bold, resolute fellows whom they were gradually bringing into the affair. For it had been decided that no less than forty men would be necessary for the undertaking as now planned if they were to make sure of succeeding in it.

There were, however, no meetings this time at the house in the Strand. Although the young Countess of Lochmore in her eagerness to serve the cause urged her brother freely to use her house, he refused to involve her in a matter so dangerous. Instead, he assembled his plotters, now at the Old King's Head in Leadenhall Street, now at the Blue Posts in Spring Gardens, now in other similar resorts.

Whilst new recruits were daily being brought to these meetings, there was one important secession. Sir John Fenwick had withdrawn as soon as it had been made clear to him that the assassination of the Prince of Orange was to be the prelude of the projected revolution.

He would shed, he announced, the last drop of his own blood to bring back King James, but he would be no party to the shedding of the blood of King William. He would keep their secret; but he would associate with them no further.

They let him go, too well aware of the stoutness of his Jacobitism, of which he had already given overwhelming proof, to fear betrayal by him.

The tale of that great Assassination Plot has been told so often that no more than the briefest summary need here be rehearsed.

It failed because of that which is ever to be apprehended when great numbers share a secret.

All was ready and each of the men participating was assigned to his post in an attack to be made upon the royal coach at Turnham Green on Saturday, the 15th February, when the King would be on his way to hunt in Richmond Park.

Some two or three days before, Porter had brought in a young Catholic gentleman from Hampshire who owed him great favours. This gentleman, William Prendergass, an ardent Jacobite, was, like Sir John Fenwick, ready enough to bear a hand in a rising but would have no part in murder. Going further than Sir John, not only would he have no part in it, but it appalled him to stand passively aside and let this thing be done.

Prendergass was torn between his Christian duty to avert the crime, and his duty to Porter, imposed by gratitude for past kindnesses, which made it impossible to betray him to the gallows. In his quandary, he finally attempted to be loyal at once to both these duties.

He went on Friday, the 14th, to Kensington, obtained an audience of the Earl of Portland, and adjured him as he valued the life of the King not to permit His Majesty to hunt upon the morrow.

He was as explicit as he dared to be, more explicit even than he need have been.

"King William," he said, "is the enemy of my religion, yet my religion constrains me to give you this caution."

Naturally, this was not enough for William Bentinck. He desired to know more; a great deal more. But Prendergass had no more to tell him.

"Ask me no questions, my lord; because I cannot answer them. Many of those in the plot are my friends, and one of them is my benefactor. Neither threats nor promises will induce me to betray their names."

At last Portland suffered him to depart, and King William did not hunt upon that Saturday, giving out that he was indisposed.

It was vexatious to the plotters who had everything prepared down to the minutest detail. Delays, Invernaion knew, were dangerous. Still, what had not been done on that day would be done upon the following Saturday.

But on the evening of the following Friday Prendergass was sent for by Portland, and by Portland introduced to the presence of the King.

Little Hooknose was very gentle with him, and used great tact.

He pointed out that the disclosure made was enough to lead him to suspect every man about him, enough to embitter his life, but not to preserve it. He confessed his obligations to Prendergass, but represented strongly to him that having said so much, he must, perforce, say more.

The Hampshire gentleman, in deepest distress, spoke of his benefactor who was one of the leading spirits in this plot, and of the impossibility of betraying him to his death. At last, when further pressed, he demanded a promise from the King that the information he could give would be used only to prevent the crime and not to destroy the criminals. King William passed him his word of honour that the information should not be used against the life of any man without the consent of Prendergass.

Then, at last, the Hampshire gentleman spoke freely. He named the plotters, and claimed, under the royal promise, the safety of Porter.

On the morrow, as on the previous Saturday, all was again prepared, each man assigned to his post in the attack. Prendergass, himself, was appointed to be one of the eight who were to fire into the coach after the Lifeguards had been surprised and routed.

But, also as on the previous Saturday, again the King did not hunt, and this time there was panic among the conspirators, for a trooper in the Blues, who was, actually privy to the plot, warned one of them, named Keyes, that there were queer rumours afloat. On the heels of this warning came news that the guards at the Palace had been doubled.

Nevertheless, Invernaion sought to rally their fainting courage. He urged them to stand fast, and, supported by Charnock, proposed that they should fall upon the King next morning as he drove out of Hyde Park on his way to chapel.

But in the early hours of that Sunday morning Charnock was arrested. Other arrests followed fast. Before noon seventeen of the conspirators were in custody, and the remainder were hunted so hard and diligently that within a few days all were taken with the exception of Invernaion and Barclay. These two, with a heavy price upon the head of each as a reward for his apprehension, had successfully eluded capture.

How they could have got away during those days when such was the vigilance that it was, almost impossible to perform a journey without a passport or to procure post-horses without the authority of a justice of the peace, remained a vexatious mystery to the government. That the authorities were in no doubt as to Invernaion's presence and share in the business was shown by a military invasion of Lochmore House. It was searched from cellar to garret. But beyond this her ladyship was not molested.

That the fugitives had got clear away was soon plain. For the government heard from their spies across the water that Invernaion and Barclay were at Calais with King James and the army mustered there, which – now that the plot had failed – would no longer embark to attempt the invasion of England.

Chapter 7

The Aftermath

A lenient government, expressing the will of a lenient monarch, was content with the execution of eight from all those conspirators who had been rounded up.

Charnock, that sometime Vice-President of Magdalen College, was among the first of these. Porter, who deserved death more than any of them, went free on the stipulation of Prendergass, and further paid for that freedom by giving evidence for the Crown against his associates. De la Rue and Cardell Goodman, following Porter's wise but unsavoury example, also saved their necks by turning informers.

The testimony of these men, among others, enabled the government to proceed vigorously against those Jacobites who whilst not directly concerned in the Assassination Plot, had nevertheless either tacitly given it their countenance or had otherwise conspired against the King de facto.

In this, the country was solidly behind the government. Out of the general horror which a plot so abominable inspired, had sprung a reaction of such popularity for King William as he had not known since he landed at Torbay in the hour of the country's need of a champion to defend it from the tyranny of James.

Among those so arrested in that aftermath were Sir John Friend and Sir John Fenwick, neither of whom had given the plot his countenance. Glenleven, suspecting that the evidence which had sent them to the Tower might also have incriminated him, had practically determined to join Invernaion across the Channel, when his own arrest took place.

It happened at the house of his kinswoman Lady Lochmore one April evening, and added to the dejection under which that misguided lady already lay in those unhappy days, a dejection which she had been bitterly expressing to him.

In her view the cause seemed definitely ruined, not only because the blow had failed, but because in failing it had actually gone to swell the credit of the usurper.

Glenleven, however, and despite anxieties on his own account, was not disposed to take so gloomy a view.

"My dear, you leave out of your reckoning the volatile inconstancy of the mob. The people are swayed emotionally at the moment; that is all. When this wave of sentiment passes, and they are face to face with stark realities again, we shall hear fewer shouts of 'long live King William.' The higher this wave of emotionalism lifts the popular mind, the deeper the trough into which it will presently sink. Be sure that this will follow. When it does, then will be our opportunity."

With a resolute smile on his thin, firm lips, he stood before her, an incarnation of virile grace, an inspiration of courage.

"I would I had your confidence," she sighed. "Meanwhile the only thing I hear are these horrible execrations of Ian's name. What do they know, who execrate him so bitterly, of the selfless devotion by which he is inspired?"

He shrugged. "That, too, will pass. Heed it no more than you heed the wind that howls under the eaves. The one is as fickle as the other."

She looked at him, and there was a kindling of admiration in her glance.

"You have no fear for yourself, Jamie, while this hunt is up?"

"Fear? No. Not fear." He spread his elegant hands. "But I have misgivings. Who enters upon a gamble must set a stake upon the board, and must be prepared to lose it."

"You are very brave."

He laughed, almost ingenuously, as if covering his pleasure in that flattering speech of one from whom he coveted flattery but seldom earned it.

"No. Not brave. Merely clear-sighted. So is King William's government. And it is to this that you may attribute such clemency as it has displayed. It will not take the risk of nauseating the public with too much blood. For that same reason it is unlikely that they will make any more victims."

He was about to add that, nevertheless, his preparations were made to go abroad for a while, that on the morrow he would be setting out, and that this was really a leave-taking visit, when her next words arrested him.

She had fetched a sigh. "I would I could be as confident as you."

He drew nearer by a step, an awakening excitement in his glance. If his peril rendered him glorious in her eyes, then in peril he would remain. As he had just observed, who gambles must set a stake upon the board, and in a game for such a prize as he accounted her, he was ready to stake all.

Not since that stormy night, now long ago, when snug in this same room the lover had peremptorily been bidden to withdraw into the kinsman, had Glenleven ventured again to suffer the lover to come forth. But though unobtrusive, that lover had ever been patiently alert, watching for an opportunity to re-emerge. That opportunity he seemed now to perceive, and he was prompt to its call.

"Why so?" he asked. "What have you to fear?"

"Your impeachment," she answered frankly.

"It gives you concern?" He was wistful.

"Do you need to ask? What should I be, Jamie, if it did not?"

He looked deep into her eyes. His wistful smile expanded, softening the harshness of his countenance. "How sweet is peril that will arouse such tender fears."

And then a knock fell upon the door, and her butler Angus entered the room. Glenleven cursed the inopportuneness of the interruption until he perceived the scared expression on the servant's face, and something more. Angus did not come alone. An officer in a red coat was on his heels. This officer came forward, brushing past the butler, whilst two troopers surged upon the threshold.

Glenleven understood, and his heart sank like a stone through water. He had delayed too long.

Her ladyship had risen in alarm, a hand at her bosom. The officer, hat in hand, was bowing low before her.

"What is this, sir?" she asked him.

"I crave your ladyship's indulgence." He straightened himself, and looked gently at Glenleven. "I have a writ for your attachment, my lord. I was told to seek you here if you were not at your own lodgings."

Glenleven had drawn himself up. He had lost a little colour; but, at least, he had recovered his momentarily shaken self-possession. There was a whimsical smile on his lips as he made an answer whose full meaning was for her ladyship alone.

"Though on such an errand you could never have been opportune, yet you could hardly arrive more inopportunely than you do. What is the charge against me, sir?"

"High treason, my lord."

"No less? Ah, well. To protest to you would be to waste your time, captain. Such things are to be borne. My sword is below, sir, at your disposal. Will you give me a moment in which to take my leave of her ladyship?"

The officer looked at him shrewdly. "You give me your word, my lord, that you will make no attempt to escape?"

"My word of honour. Why should I escape? I shall be as well lodged in the Tower as elsewhere, and I can assure you that I have nothing to apprehend beyond that."

"I trust so, indeed, my lord." The officer bowed. His tone changed to curtness. "Make the most of five minutes."

He withdrew with Angus; the door closed; and Glenleven and her ladyship were left alone together.

She flew to him at once, and set her hands on his shoulders.

"Jamie!" she cried. The consternation which had blanched her cheek and dilated those deep blue eyes left her no words beyond that piteous ejaculation of his name.

His voice and manner were very soft and tender.

"Nay, sweet!" Soothingly his fingers stroked her lustrous black hair. "Nay! I am not on Tower Hill yet. And by God's help and yours I never shall be."

"By my help? By mine?" She seemed to ask him did he mock her.

His fingers paused in their caress. He gripped both her wrists and held them, her hands still upon his shoulders.

"Listen," he bade her sharply, in a sudden excitement. "Listen carefully. The thought has only just occurred to me: providentially, perhaps, before it is too late. The law requires two witnesses before it can convict a man of treason. If I had but thought of it sooner I might have provided. Of all those who could have witnessed against me only two remain alive, saving Fenwick, who is himself under arrest and moreover quite dependable. Those two witnesses, however, are both informers: that blackguard Porter, and that other blackguard de la Rue. If by bribery or otherwise either of them could be induced to leave the country, the government would be powerless to proceed with my impeachment. Porter dare not go. That arch-Judas knows that his life would not be worth a moment's purchase out of England. But with de la Rue it is different. He is French, and at a price he might be glad to repatriate himself. Will you send for him and see what you can do? He is commonly to be found at the Blue Posts. If you can induce him to leave England, I am safe. Whatever you find it necessary to spend I will refund as soon as…"

"Leave that," she interrupted sharply. "Whatever the cost, Jamie, it shall be done, if it can be done. And it will be money spent for the cause."

"Ah, no!"

"Ah, yes! I can afford it. You cannot. No need for pretences between us, Jamie."

"We'll talk of this again. I may not stay now. Have courage, my dear. Fear nothing. God keep you safe."

He kissed her for the first time. And considering in what case he stood, and how soon, in spite of all that she could do, those lips might be cold, she did not refuse him hers.

His eyes were very tender, his smile very gentle. "Thus I am made strong," he said, and loosed her wrists.

When he was gone she lost no time. Not only did she send one of her trusty Macdonald footmen to the Blue Posts in Spring Gardens with a note requesting Monsieur de la Rue to wait upon her at the earliest moment, but she sent another riding down to Romney Marsh, to the sequestered house of the smuggler Hunt, who was always ready to handle Jacobite contraband. The servant bore a letter for Invernaion, which Hunt was to smuggle across the Channel with the utmost dispatch. It conveyed to her brother, in the cipher that she used with him, the bare fact of Glenleven's arrest.

That done, she sat down to wait for Monsieur de la Rue.

Chapter 8

Monsieur de la Rue

Monsieur de la Rue kept her ladyship waiting for three days.

By the time he appeared she was almost distracted by impatience and anxiety.

He came with a swagger, a man of forty, of middle height, lean everywhere save at the waist, where he exhibited the beginnings of a paunch. His dress with its tarnished lace displayed a tawdry attempt at modishness. His cheap brown wig looked as if it had come from a tub in Rosemary Lane. His mean eyes were bleary, his face mottled, save where the razor had left his cheeks blue-black.

On being introduced, and finding himself alone with her ladyship, he simpered and made a very elaborate leg, sweeping the floor with the limp feather in his black castor. In her memory he had already been unprepossessing; in actual fact she found him now, at these close quarters, grotesquely repulsive.

"Madame!" He bowed. "Ma reine!" He bowed again. "To serve you. Your most humble obedient." He bowed yet a third time, more profoundly than ever. "You send for me. Oh, but I am so honoured. I come like the wind. I am here."

"God knows you are," said her ladyship, with the suspicion of a sniff. "But nothing like the wind, save in your wordiness." Sharply she added: "It is three days since I sent for you."

59

"You conceive that I delayed? Oh!" His tone conveyed the pain he suffered under such an imputation. Then he laughed it to utter scorn. "Oh, that! Three days! Que Dieu me damne! You think I make you wait three days? You think my own impatience wait so long? Not three minutes, milady, from the instant your command is in my hands. I come at once."

She liked neither his leer, nor the ardour in his little eyes.

"Sit down," she said, and her tone was one of command rather than of invitation.

"Madame permits?" He hitched his sword forward, and sank into a chair, placing his hat on the floor beside him.

"There is a service I require of you, Monsieur de la Rue."

"I am the most fortunate of men. It will be a happiness to serve milady."

"It will also be profitable."

"Oh, that!" De la Rue waved a scornful hand. "I listen."

"What interest keeps you in England, Monsieur?"

Surprise at the question was reflected in his blotchy face. He took time to answer, and in that time his eyes considered her from head to foot with an appraising glance that turned her hot with shame. In self-defence she increased the haughty peremptoriness of her manner. She tapped the floor with her foot. "Well, sir? Is the question difficult to answer?"

"It is not so easy," he said, and smirked. "It is not nice to kiss and tell. No? Oh, but I will be frank with you. Enfin! I am of a susceptibility, milady. Romantic! It is my weakness. And so, while I love France, I am kept here by this so tender heart." He placed in the region of it a hand that was none too clean. "First there was Madame la Duchesse de Cleveland. Beautiful woman, oh, but so exigent, that one. Then there was Milady Belcastle." He was ticking them off on his fingers. "Next come... "

She cut him short, angrily contemptuous. "Lord, man! Do I want a catalogue of your good fortunes?"

He opened his mouth in surprise, to show a row of sound if yellowish teeth. His tone was aggrieved.

"But it is the explanation that madame requested. The explanation of why I continue in exile."

"I see," she answered tartly. "I hope that such strong reasons as these are now all in the past, and that you have no such bond to hold you here at present."

"Oho! But have I not, milady? Never so strong a bond as now."

Mastering her repugnance she made an effort to look into that sly, leering face. She concluded that his low cunning had guessed her aim and that he was making difficulties so as to increase the price.

"Faugh! Will a thousand pounds break the bond?"

Watching him as she spoke, she perceived that she had startled him. Some of the fire perished in his countenance. He meditatively stroked his chin, then left his hand to screen his mouth. Between the blotches his cheeks had turned ashen.

From these signs she knew that she had offered too much; that by the magnitude of the sum offered she had betrayed the magnitude of her need.

"A thousand pounds, milady!" he said in a sepulchral voice. "But a thousand pounds for what?"

"To take yourself off to France at once, and stay there."

He continued to stare for some seconds. At last he uncovered his mouth and disclosed the grin that curled it. He was himself again.

"I understand, I think." He slowly winked at her. "There are things I could tell. Inconvenient things, is it not? Things which might cost some lives. Oh yes. And for this a thousand pounds?"

"Five hundred down, and five hundred to be paid to you by my brother in France when you are there."

He hunched his shoulders. "It might be. Yes, it might be." His tone was reflective. "But it is dangerous in France for me. Very dangerous. You see, I am here because in France I kill a man once. Oh, but in a duel. In honour. I am a great swordsman. So all was fair. But this man's family is noble, and they complain to the King. They will move my process. Perhaps it is not yet forgot. You see the danger, milady?"

"You need not stay in France. You need not even go there. There are other countries where a man of your enterprise should prosper. All that I really require of you is that you leave England."

"But where shall I go if not to France? Must I live expatriate all my life? Here in England I am habituated now, and I can live. But where else? In Italy?" His grimace repudiated the idea. "In Spain? Oh, that!"

Again she perceived here no more than tactics to advance the price of his consent. And from extreme anxiety fell, herself, into the worst of tactical errors.

"To compensate you I would raise the figure. See: I will double it. What do you say now?"

His eyes were smouldering as they pondered her again. He sighed and the fawning note in his voice increased when he replied.

"Milady, no man could resist to do your pleasure. I least of all men, ma reine. What is it to me that I put my life in peril, so that I serve you?"

She strove with her nausea. "You agree, then?"

"Oh! But should I not agree?" He leaned towards her, his eyes hideously liquid, his voice softened, pleading and oily. "I only ask, ma reine, that you add a mark of your favour."

"Of my favour?" she frowned. "What better mark than this two thousand pounds?"

He continued to ogle her, leering, for a long moment before he spoke. It was almost as if in the silence he would communicate his thought, by the force of it, directly to her mind. Then, as she made no sign, he gave it utterance.

"Something the sweet memory of which would give me strength and courage in my last hours if I have to pay with my life for having done your pleasure."

The fixed stare of her eyes in that white face were a sufficient evidence of her suspicion and her horror. Yet in a toneless voice she said: "I do not understand."

He shifted on his chair. He sat further forward, so that by leaning over he might just have touched her. "Is it so difficult then, to understand? Oh, I am poor yes. I am misfortunate. And so I cannot make the big gesture and refuse your two thousand pounds. Yet not for two thousand, not for twenty thousand pounds alone would I do this thing. But for love... For love, ah yes, my queen."

He propelled himself still further, and suddenly was down on one knee at her feet, reaching out hands to paw her.

She sprang up instantly, less in anger than in such a feeling as must have been hers if in the public street someone had bespattered her with ordures.

"God!" she choked, as she thrust her chair backwards to make room for her recoil.

But Monsieur de la Rue continued to kneel before her, with bowed head and outflung arms. "What do I ask that should so affright you?"

"You do not frighten me, monsieur. That is not at all the word."

"Not the word? What word, then?" But he did not await her answer. He ran torrentially on. "I pay perhaps with my life for what is to do. And I am glad to pay. Oh, yes. If I give that, I give all. Don't you understand? Will you not, then, be generous, too, with me?"

"Get up, man. Go!"

But he merely looked up from his knees in hurt surprise. He saw her standing erect there, forbidding, majestic, all cold and self-contained, save that the tumult in her alluring breast betrayed her inward agitation.

He shrugged and flung out his arms again, clicking his tongue against the roof of his mouth. "Bien!" He got slowly to his feet.

But his resignation was by no means that of despair. She had betrayed her need to be so terribly compelling that no price within her means could be too high. Thus, at least, the rascal read her. "I see. I am abrupt, is it not? I take you by surprise. It was to have been foreseen." He sighed. "I go now. Yes. But I come again. Perhaps tomorrow. You will think of what I say. No? You will come to see that if I risk my life... "

"Oh, go," she angrily exploded, and stepping past him to the fireplace pulled the bell-cord.

From the threshold, when Angus held the door for him, he threw her a congé, and the leer on his face was of unabated confidence.

"A bientôt, ma reine!"

He waited three whole days before presenting himself again. In this his patience was that of calculation. He accounted himself very experienced in the operations of the human heart; and his experience told him that to ensure himself a welcome he must bring this lady, whose need of him he had gauged to be so obviously and desperately urgent, to the point of fearing that he might not come again. The fear that a chance has been lost is a seed of bitter regret from which future wisdom may spring.

The promptitude with which he was admitted confirmed him. The austerity with which the lady received him he supposed to be assumed.

He bowed, fantastically as ever, when they were alone.

"Me voici, ma reine. I said I should return. I am here to do your service."

"At my price, Monsieur de la Rue?"

"At your price. Oh, yes. Assuredly at your price. And also at mine."

She had remained seated to receive him, and intended so to remain, with the fellow standing before her throughout the interview. Thus she would mark the difference in their stations, and of that difference make a barrier against his ineffable impertinences. But at his last words her resolve was forgotten. She sprang to her feet, quivering with indignation. She spoke in a choking voice.

"Insolent dog! I will have you whipped from my door."

He laughed. He shrugged. He flourished himself. He set a hand on his pummel and his head on one side to regard her. "Words, and a woman's. We have a proverb in France that a woman's tongue does no dishonour. So I am not angry. No, no. I understand. But you waste time. Consider, my queen, that you have no choice. Oh, yes. A choice: to let this poor milord Glenleven be convicted of high treason, and then... " He drew a hand edgewise across his throat. "Bon soir! He is dear to you, this good milord Glenleven. Because he is dear to you I will risk my life to save him. Does not that deserve all that a woman, a great lady, can give? Oh, madame! You think perhaps, because I am like this, that we are not equals. Because you see me poor, you think that I am a roturier. Ah that! Look at me. Yes, look at me well." He drew himself up, and threw back his head in its cheap, ill-kempt wig. "Me, I am noble. That jumps to the eye. The beautiful Madame la Duchesse de Cleveland..."

He was allowed to get no further. She had been looking at him as he invited her, but with eyes that held only disgust. She had mastered, not her anger, but the heat of it.

"Noble! De la Rue in name, and de la rue, in fact. A nobleman of the streets, of the kennels. It is finished! Go! I do not need your service."

"You do not..." His mouth opened in astonishment. Then it closed with a snap. "Peste! You play comedy with me. You want to laugh. Why, you never needed a man's service more."

"Angus!"

The call was answered with a promptitude that startled the Frenchman.

"The door! Monsieur de la Rue to the door!"

Monsieur de la Rue made a great display of dignity. He drew himself almost on to his toes. His left hand pressing on his hilt, thrust the sword horizontally behind him. He was white with rage.

"To the door, eh? Monsieur de la Rue to the door, eh? It is as you would say, madame, milord Glenleven to the scaffold."

In her changed expression he thought he saw that at last he had really touched her; thought that she had caught, as indeed she had, in his mocking tone the threat that he would precipitate the doom she sought to bribe him to avert.

"Stay," she said. She put a hand to her brow. Then she waved Angus out again. "Wait, Angus."

The servant withdrew, wooden of face, but alert of eye.

"Listen, Monsieur de la Rue, I am sorry for what I said."

Instantly he melted. "Not another word, madame. The regret mends all. We are going to talk reasonably. Like two good friends. Yes?"

"I am going to offer you," she said slowly, "three thousand pounds to do as I require. It is a fortune, Monsieur de la Rue. You will accept?"

He thought her almost piteous in her eagerness. He bowed a little.

"Oh, yes. I will accept. I had already accepted less. But could I be so ungallant as to forgo what I prize above all the gold of Peru? Ah, fi donc! What should I be then, eh?"

Involuntarily the words broke from her. "What should I be?"

"You, milady? Oh! The Duchess of Cleveland... "

"Silence, man. Have you no decency at all?"

"Decency!" He was momentarily lost in amazement. Then he thought he understood. "Ah! You fear I talk. Because I tell you of the beautiful Barbara, and of Milady Belcastle, and so on, you think I talk too much. You think... "

"Silence, you foul coxcomb! Be silent, do you hear?" She was suddenly all imperiousness: a great lady speaking to an impertinent lackey. Her tone and mien dominated him in spite of himself.

"If you dare to speak again except to say yes or no, I'll have you whipped till the blood runs from your back. Keep your hands from that sword, fool. It won't avail you against the whips of my grooms, and they are within call. I'll have no heroics from you, my man. Now then. I have offered you a sum of money upon certain terms. Do you accept or not?"

He stood silent, ashen-faced, his eyes that had ogled so adoringly holding now only malevolence. Thus for a long moment before he spoke.

"If I accept, you pay me the half at once, you said?"

"I said so. Yes. That was before I understood with what a rat I am dealing. You shall be paid when the service is rendered, when you are safely abroad; and you shall be paid in instalments to keep you honest for the necessary time; in instalments of five hundred pounds a year."

He was surprised and indignant. "Oh that! How do I answer that?" he was beginning, with a resumption of his earlier insolence.

But she checked him instantly. "You will answer it just yes or no. That's all."

He broke out violently, snarling like a threatened cur. "Then no, no, no, mille fois. Goddam! No."

"Angus!" was her instant call, and instantly again Angus appeared.

She waved an eloquent hand, turned her back upon Monsieur de la Rue, and moved down the room with a leisurely grace, as if concerned no further.

"Milady!" said the Frenchman.

But she took no heed. It was Angus who spoke next, peremptorily, from the door, which he was holding. "Come, mossoo. Out of here!"

To Monsieur de la Rue this was the end of the world. He could not believe that it was real. He showed his teeth in a livid grin. Even his blotches had paled. He did not actually spit, but he made a sound that simulated the act, and on that turned and moved heavy-footed to the door.

He crossed the threshold, and disappeared into the dimly lighted hall. Uproar followed instantly.

Within the room her ladyship stood tense, listening, a smile, faintly mocking, on her white face.

Monsieur de la Rue's bellowing voice came charged with wild rage.

"Trahison! Sacrée canaille! Trahison!"

The outcry was followed by sounds of panting, of grunting, of a smothered laugh or two, of slither of receding feet, and then a distant muttering.

After a moment Angus re-entered. He wore a half-repressed grin.

"The carle craves word wi' your ladyship."

She nodded. "Bring him in."

He came, propelled by two stalwart Macdonalds, a sorry spectacle. He was without hat or wig or sword; his coat was torn from shoulder to waist; his neckcloth was in disorder and his face inflamed; his hands were tied behind him, and his ankles so hobbled that he could little more than stand. He foamed at the lips as he addressed her ladyship.

"You think this will serve, milady? You think I am such a fool as to come into this danger without my little precautions? Ha!" He laughed savagely. "Ah that! Not me. I give you warning. If I do not return to my friends they will know where to find me."

She smiled upon him, exasperatingly tranquil.

"If that were true," she said, "you would be safe only so long as you did not warn me of it. Then your friends would have a chance of finding you. You are a fool, de la Rue. But not such a fool as not to realize that. If it were true you would not dare to take the risk of your friends not finding you when they came. You would reflect, and reflecting you would remember that the river runs at the bottom of my garden. It is only a poor cozener who would be so rashly foolish as to threaten. Be thankful that I perceive it.

"Take him away, Angus, and bestow him in the cellar, to cool. His humours are a little ardent."

They dragged him unceremoniously out, spitting threats and blasphemies.

Chapter 9

Invernaion's Raids

It was four days after that safe bestowal of Monsieur de la Rue in the cellar of Lochmore House when Ian Macdonald arrived in London in answer to his sister's appeal. Her messenger had made good speed, and he, himself, had made even better, spurred by generous anxiety for his kinsman.

He came accompanied by a young Irish officer, named O'Brien, who had been at the Boyne and at Limerick and who had elected at the end to go overseas with Sarsfield.

Never was Ian more welcome to his sister, whose anxieties increased with every day that the amorous Frenchman spent in her cellar.

She informed both Ian and his companion of Glenleven's situation and his need: how he could be made safe by the elimination of one of the only two witnesses against him. But it was to Ian alone that she related the full circumstances in which she came to hold de la Rue a captive.

He was inflamed with anger at the monstrous story.

"I marvel you could have practised such self-restraint; that you did not bid them tie a stone to his neck and cast him into the river. It is done every day with curs less foul."

Gradually, however, his seething rage gave way to mirth at the picture his mind evoked of the Frenchman's ultimate discomfiture.

O'Brien was brought in and informed, with certain omissions, that de la Rue was here under their hand.

The young Irishman chuckled his delight and regarded the slim, stately Countess with eyes of adoring wonder.

"Ye've contrived it finely. Faith, it's a man's heart your ladyship carries in that lovely breast. It's behind the fair we are, Macdonald. The thing is done already."

"Not quite," said Invernaion. "He can't be left here."

"To be sure not." The young Irishman was standing by the window whence he could view the sloping garden and the river. "And isn't the water handy. The tide'll carry the blackguard comfortably to sea."

Invernaion shook his head. "No," he said. "We'll have to take him back with us over the water."

"Sure, now, wouldn't he be safer under it? But as ye please. Since we have him here to our hand we need lose no time about it."

But again Invernaion did not agree. "There's Ailsa," he objected. "I'll not have her needlessly compromised. If it were to become known..."

"How should it?" she interrupted. "And what matter if it did?"

"Setting aside that you're my sister, and that I love you, you're too valuable to us. And no suspicion must fall on you that would diminish that value. It's bad enough that you should have a marked man like me for a brother." He slipped an arm about her waist, drew her to him and kissed her cheek.

"My use here is the only reason against which I will not argue. But if you don't take him from here, where he is helpless, what then?"

"I'll take him elsewhere, never fear. And I shall see that it's known that I've taken him. That will make you safe. Meanwhile be sure that I shall not let him out of my sight when he leaves your house."

"Aren't you taking an unnecessary risk, Ian?"

"Risk? I hope I may never face a worse."

They dined in comfort as the day was fading. At dusk they took their leave.

"In five minutes' time you may let this Frenchman loose," said Ian.

No sooner had they departed than she sent Angus to fetch the prisoner.

De la Rue, fierce as a newly caged hawk, reared himself on his pallet to glare at them.

"Well, my Scots jackals? Has the she-cat come to her senses?"

"Come out of that," said Angus. "I'm to show you the door."

"The door?" Monsieur de la Rue almost feared that he was being mocked.

"Ay, we're sick o' the sight of your blotchy face. So be stirring now."

De la Rue came to his feet. "Am I to see milady?"

"Ye're not. Her ladyship's seen too much of you already. Come on."

"Listen, my friend. You will tell her ladyship that it will be good for her friend that she see me again. And bad – very bad – for him if she do not."

"My orders," said the stolid Angus, "are to show you the door."

"But, my friend… "

"I am not your friend. To Hell with your impudence. Here, my lads, help him out."

Protesting to the last, they dragged him above and thrust him ignominiously from the door.

When it had closed upon him he shook his fist at it, and cursed, virulently and profusely, all whom it sheltered.

Then, with dragging feet, he went raging down the steps, across the flagged courtyard, to the tall wrought-iron gate that opened upon the Strand. He passed out and clanged the gate furiously after him. Then he stood, in the dusk, undecided which way to turn his steps.

There were few wayfarers about at that hour, and most of these were moving briskly. But near the eastern end of the railings that enclosed her ladyship's courtyard, two men, who might have met by chance, stood idly chatting and laughing together.

De la Rue took at last his decision. He turned to the right, and went off quickly, brushing past those loiterers. He never looked behind him as he made off. But even had he done so it is unlikely that they would have allowed him to perceive that they were following.

He made his way towards the Fleet. A little beyond Temple Bar he dived into an alley on the right that ran down towards the river. Midway in this an open doorway flung a rhomb of yellow light across the narrow way in which night had already fallen. De la Rue's figure was for a moment a black silhouette in this patch of light. Then he had vanished through the open doorway of the Crowing Cock.

A full five minutes later two gentlemen of a quality rarely seen in that haunt stood in the inn's flagged passage, and the taller of the twain beckoned the vintner from the tap-room.

"Have you a room at hand where we can be private?" The speaker displayed a guinea.

The vintner blinked, received with bowed back that golden token of good will, and ushered them at once into a small room beyond the tap.

"Your worships'll be private in here, and cosy. What may I serve you?"

The tall dark stranger assumed a confidential manner. "I have cause to believe that a Monsieur de la Rue is in your house. I have a word of particular importance for him. Will you ask him to wait on me here?"

The vintner, a lanky, evil-looking fellow, whose proper place seemed to be within the Liberties of Whitefriars, rather than just without them, looked searchingly at his visitor.

"I am not sure as there's anyone here o' that name. What was it, did ye say?"

"De la Rue. And I know that he is here, because I chanced to see him enter. A very fortunate chance for him and for me. I'll be obliged to you, landlord."

The vintner went out, closing the door. There was a pause, and then, at last, steps on the flags of the passage, which came to a halt at the door. Another pause, and abruptly the door was flung open.

Monsieur de la Rue stood on the threshold, raking the room with a mistrustful eye. He saw only O'Brien, who directly confronted him. Invernaion had taken up such a position that the door as it opened made a screen for him.

O'Brien advanced a step with an inviting smile.

"Come in with you, Monsieur de la Rue. Sure it's the luckiest chance now for both of us that I should light upon you in this way. Just as I was after wondering where I could be finding ye. Come you in, then. Come in, and close the door."

Seeing only one man, be his disarming amiability genuine or not, the mystified de la Rue did as he was bidden, and turned to close the door. In the act of doing so he uncovered the man whom it concealed. He started violently, checked, looked closely, and loosed a panic-stricken outcry.

"Invernaion!"

That name, which recent events had rendered famous, reverberated through the mean house, followed almost at once by the bang of the door, as Ian Macdonald thrust his weight against it to close it completely.

Before de la Rue could move, the muzzle of a pistol was rammed hard into his stomach, and the young Scot was mildly warning him.

"Another sound, my poodle, and I'll drill a hole in your guts that will ruin your digestion for ever." He paused there, smiling cruelly into that villainous, scared face. "Be sensible, and no harm shall come to you beyond a little jaunt with me and my friend."

De la Rue, watchful of eye, passed a tongue over his lips to moisten them.

"What do you want with me?" His tone was defiant.

"Superfluous question! Search your memory of recent events. You'll find the answer there. You were offered as much as three thousand pounds to take a journey. You would not accept. You will take that journey now for the sheer love of your life, and so as to preserve it. All I desire, de la Rue, is your elimination, and I'll not hesitate to eliminate you finally. If you want to avoid that, you can do it by un-resisting obedience." Without turning his head he spoke to O'Brien. "Philip! The door, if you please. And lead the way."

They went out processionally, O'Brien leading, de la Rue following and Ian Macdonald coming last, thrusting the Frenchman onward with the muzzle of the pistol, pressed now into his back.

In the passage they met the gaping landlord and a tapster.

"Give way there if you would be avoiding trouble," said the Irishman.

The vintner, seeing no reason to risk a bullet, was so prudent as to obey, and offered no obstacle to their departure. But as soon as he judged it safe to do so, he ran off to inform the nearest justice that that Jacobite traitor Invernaion had raided his house and carried off Monsieur de la Rue under threats of violence.

There was a fine stir that very night. Whitehall was in consternation. Even sedate Kensington was agitated. Order was promptly taken. The ports were closed. But too late. Invernaion had an ample start. The cutter that had brought him over waited at Greenwich, and he was well out at sea before the messengers were galloping with orders to stop him.

For a fortnight Invernaion's Raid, as the affair was called, was the talk of the town. It was discussed with anger at such coffee-houses as the Rose and Garraway's, and with laughter at the Old King's Head in Leadenhall Street. That infant newspaper, the *English Courant*, contained in four successive issues little more than indignant leading articles on the subject. By the last of these its readers were informed of intelligence from France according to which Monsieur de la Rue had been handed over by the audacious Invernaion to French justice, which had long been seeking him for an affair which he described as a duel, but which the French authorities regarded as a murder. This man whose testimony on certain Jacobite matters was so valuable to King William's government had been cast into the Bastille and would probably never be heard of again.

As the matter was, at last, beginning to grow stale, interest in it was revived by the reappearance in public of my Lord Glenleven. He had been restored to liberty by a government which realized that the effective suppression of one of the only two witnesses against him made it impossible to bring him to trial.

On the day after his release he waited upon Lady Lochmore. He came, of course, to return thanks. But he came also, and with confidence, for something more. He came to resume that conversation so inopportunely interrupted. He was to learn, however, how different are the emotions excited by the case of a man who stands in peril of death from those aroused by one who is secure.

He went with gay confidence into her ladyship's presence, looking his best, his slight elegant figure set off by a coat of royal blue that was richly laced with gold. He almost ran to her, with a deep-throated cry of "Ailsa!"

Having kissed her at parting, it seemed to him proper that a kiss should mark this happy reunion. In some such state of mind she, too, may have suffered that warm salute.

Then he held her by the shoulders, at arm's length, and out of a radiant countenance surveyed her.

"I owe you so much, my Ailsa," he cried. "My life, no less."

"You owe it to Ian."

The quick disclaimer and something chilly in her voice and manner momentarily dimmed his radiance.

"To you and Ian, if you will," he insisted. "God knows I do not forget his part in this. But neither can I permit you to diminish your own. I owe my life to you both. To you I will repay the debt, my Ailsa, by a life of such devotion as you have never dreamed of."

Quietly she disengaged her shoulder from his fond grip. She drew away a little. "You make too much of it, Jamie. There is no debt. To a kinsman it was no more than a duty that we performed. And certainly we claim no payment."

He strove with her coyness, as he supposed it. "Though you may not claim it, it shall be made, my dear."

He approached her again. Again she drew back.

"If you would really pay, you will pay best by never alluding to it."

Perceiving and interpreting his discomfited air, she judged it proper to leave him in no doubt whatever of her frame of mind. "That is my wish, Jamie. My definite wish. You understand. You will save me, I hope, the need of saying more."

He understood, and discomfiture deepened to utter misery in his countenance. "You bring me back to life only to deal me death."

She smiled wanly. "Jamie! Jamie! Why will you talk so, as if you lived in a romance?"

"I thought I did. It was life to me. Oh, Ailsa!"

She shook her head. "I know my mind. I doubt if I shall wed again."

He looked at her dejectedly. "I would make you so happy, Ailsa."

"So Lochmore promised."

That stung him. "You compare me with him?"

"No, Jamie. No. I mean that it would need more than a promise to persuade me into marriage."

"Do you find no more in me?"

"No more, Jamie."

"You may in time."

"Do not waste your hopes on that. Let us talk of other things. Sit. And tell me how you have fared."

He surrendered at last, his will beaten down by her quiet firmness. But he was dull on the subject of his captivity and of this release of his which just then was supplying a subject for so much gossip.

If, however, the matter of his escape had ceased, as he romantically pretended to Lady Lochmore, to be of interest to him, it was of interest to many others, and to none more than to Sir John Fenwick, still languishing in the Tower. To him it was an inspiration. As Glenleven had saved himself, so might he.

It arose out of this, that a few days later Lady Lochmore was sought by Lady Mary Fenwick, Sir John's wife. Already that poor distressed lady had flung herself at the feet of King William and had presented a petition for her husband's life. His Majesty had gently replied that it should be considered, but that the matter was one of public concern; an answer which did not seem to her to hold much promise.

If she did not cast herself at the feet of Lady Lochmore, she flung her arms about her ladyship's neck and with tears implored her to invoke Invernaion's help for Sir John as he had so nobly and ably given it to Glenleven.

"We have tried," said the comely afflicted wife, "to help ourselves. I employed a man to bribe Porter. Porter, that false scoundrel, took the money I offered – three hundred pounds – and then cheated me by handing my agent over to the justices. There remains Goodman, who is the other witness against Sir John. I dare not run the risk of a like failure with him. For then all hope would be lost. But if he were served as de la Rue was served, that would make Sir John as safe as my Lord Glenleven now is."

"Why, then, don't you so serve him?"

"Whom can I find in England to undertake it? Don't you see, Ailsa dear, that it needs someone from overseas, someone who already dare not live in England while William of Orange is King."

"You mean, in short, Invernaion?"

"Oh, Ailsa, I'ld not importune you so if I could look elsewhere."

Ailsa Lochmore was torn between distress for her friend and concern for her brother.

"You realize the peril that Ian incurs every time he enters England. You realize that this peril grows more and more acute; that there is a heavy reward offered for his arrest, and that if he is taken nothing in the world can save him. My dear, I grieve for you, oh so deeply. But Ian is my brother, and I… " She made a little helpless gesture with her hands.

They were instantly caught by Lady Mary. "I know, dear Ailsa. I know. But Ian is bold and clever and resourceful. And it is for the cause, dear. Sir John is a valued servant of King James. His life is of consequence to England. Oh what else can I say? If you fail me, Ailsa, he is lost. And I love him so, my dear. It will kill me if he perishes."

Lady Lochmore melted to the wife's distress. She took her to her bosom. "Comfort you. I will send word to Ian. I do not say that he will come. It will be for him to decide. But if I know Ian, I know what his decision will be."

"I will pray God to watch over him in this enterprise," was the fervent answer. "And I will pray God to bless you, too, Ailsa. I will pray. It is all a woman is fit for at such times. Prayers and tears."

And so it befell. Whilst still his last exploit was vividly in the memory of the town, whilst the placards were still everywhere to be seen offering two thousand pounds reward for information that would lead to the capture of Ian Macdonald of Invernaion, he reappeared again abruptly in London, accompanied as before by Philip O'Brien. And almost as abruptly as he came did he depart again, carrying off Cardell Goodman much as he had carried off de la Rue, but with less violence. Goodman accepted a bribe to depart. At the same time, so as to make sure that he earned the money, Invernaion insisted that the fellow should go with him, and so got him safely out of England and across the Channel.

This time the popular uproar and the indignation of the government were loud indeed. It was intolerable that authority should be flouted and the ends of justice thwarted in this contemptuous manner by an insolent Jacobite.

This indignation expressed itself most eloquently in the sudden raising to five thousand pounds of the reward for the apprehension of Ian Macdonald of Invernaion.

Safe across the Channel, Invernaion could laugh at this. In the Tower Sir John Fenwick, too, could laugh, and did, accounting that the government had once again been effectively checkmated, and that his enlargement was assured, impeachment being now impossible for lack of evidence. Lady Mary laughed and cried at once when she came to thank Lady Lochmore for the great service her brother had rendered.

But they rejoiced too soon.

The government could not tolerate that it should be continually cheated in this manner of the power to deal justice upon men whose guilt admitted of no doubt. Soon, in connection with Sir John, the ominous words Bill of Attainder began to be heard. That bill was moved and passed in spite of all that his friends in Parliament and out of it could do; and the end of that story is that Sir John suffered for his treason on Tower Hill.

The event shook my Lord Glenleven's sense of security. It thrust him out of his romantic pretence that life had ceased to interest him. So far did he forget the tragic role of the hopeless lover sighing for death that it was actually to Lady Lochmore that he went to confide his fears. She sought to give him courage.

"Your case is not as Sir John's. Your treasons were never as open and flagrant. Against him, too, there was the memory of a public insult to Queen Mary, which William of Orange would not be likely ever to forget or forgive. That may be why the law was so violently strained against him. It is not to be supposed that it would be so violently strained against you even had you not already been set at liberty."

"My being at liberty need not count for much. The question is, should I use this liberty to cross the Channel while there is time?"

"If you are uneasy, you might so purchase peace of mind. You have little to risk by contumacy."

He laughed sourly. "Little? Faith, I have nothing, as you should know. I don't own very much more at any time than the clothes I stand in. Yet I should detest to be forced to leave England."

His eloquent hungry eyes, intently upon her, gave her the reason plainly. Her utter unresponsiveness may have led him to add: "But I'll consider it."

He was still considering when a message reached him ordering him at once to wait upon Lord Portland at Kensington. To Sir Hamish Stuart, of Meorach, who was with him when he received the command, he expressed the melancholy opinion that once again he had waited too long. Go to Kensington now he must. There was no help for it. Although it was very likely, he dolefully opined, that from Kensington he would journey back to the Tower.

This, his gloomy prognostic, however, was not realized. It was known that at Kensington Palace he was closeted for two full hours by the clock with my Lord of Portland. But he afterwards boasted that although questioned and cross-questioned to weariness in that time, he had successfully baffled that Dutch creature of King William's.

And this would appear to be the truth, since he quitted Kensington Palace a free man.

Chapter 10

Colonel Walton's Leave-taking

Colonel Dudley Walton sauntered with Invernaion on the noble terrace of Saint Germains.

Although March was scarcely in, the sun shone with warmth from a cloudless sky, and so clear was the air that the distant spires of Paris were plainly visible from those heights.

In the years of waiting for the hour to strike in which he might actively serve his King, the Colonel had retained in the French army the commission, the duties of which he had discharged with such distinction at Namur, at Steinkirk and elsewhere. Although a well known figure at Saint Germains, it was only in the intervals of that service, and chiefly when the army was in winter quarters, that he had been seen there.

But all this was now at an end. The long-drawn war was over. Colonel Walton had resigned the commission which he had lately held under Villeroy, that feeble successor to the great Luxembourg, and he had come to Saint Germains this time to resign something more. He was really there on a visit of valediction.

His uncle, a fox-hunting Wiltshire squire, had lately died, and Dudley Walton had inherited an estate which if small and partly encumbered, sufficed, he announced, for his comparatively modest needs. He, therefore, proposed to cross to England, make his peace with King William's government, and abandoning the roving life of a soldier of fortune, settle down peacefully to the cultivation of his acres.

"I admire," said Invernaion, "the loyal frankness that brings you to confess your intentions to His Majesty. That is what I should expect in you, Dudley, once you have taken this resolve. What I should not have expected is the resolve itself."

"I disappoint you," said the Colonel.

"To be frank, and because you are my friend, you do. You not only disappoint, you bewilder me. I don't understand."

The Colonel halted, and Invernaion halted with him. They leaned upon the parapet by which they had been sauntering. Fifty paces away a lady and a gentleman were moving briskly towards them.

"Do you understand, Ian, that few things happen here that are not reported at Kensington; that every coming and going is observed by spying eyes, and communicated at once to King William's government?"

"You ask me that? Me?" Invernaion laughed without joy. "Does any man understand it better? It is only here at Saint Germains that I account myself safe nowadays from the agents of the Prince of Orange. When I leave here I have to go under an assumed name, so as to escape the attentions of those who are on the watch for me from the moment that I am out of this." He spoke so, as if reproachfully to stress the difference between Dudley Walton's case and his own. "But what is that to the matter?"

"Something, if you consider it." The Colonel was smiling.

"Damn your enigmas, Dudley. Be plain."

"On some other occasion. Here is Sir Percy Lawrence with his lady; to reproach me, I think."

Sir Percy who was frowning upon the Colonel was near enough to have overheard.

"I'd not venture quite so much, Colonel Walton. But I confess to amazement at the news I hear of you."

He was a fleshy, pompous, florid man in the forties, by much the senior of the dark, attractive lady who hung upon his arm.

The Colonel doffed his hat to them, and remained uncovered.

"Yet what matter is there for amazement? I have had ten years – ten hard years – of soldiering. I grow old... "

"Oh, Colonel! Old!" simpered the lady.

"Old enough, at least, to settle in life, now that fate gives me the opportunity. Inheritance has its duties, ma'am."

"And your duty to the King, then?" quoth Sir Percy, tartly.

"This is desertion, Colonel," the lady added, but without tartness.

"What do I desert? What prospects really remain of a restoration?" He shrugged and sighed, the natural melancholy of his countenance deepening. "When last year's hopes failed, it seemed, indeed, that the end was reached. Nothing since encourages belief – alas! – that King James will need my sword. In France, now that the war is ended, I can find no employment. Shall I, then, stay to eat King James' bread in idleness?"

Sir Percy blew out his florid cheeks. "I protest, sir, that you have no cause for such lack of faith."

"A matter of opinion, sir."

The knight's bulging eyes considered him without affection. "Do you propose to take the oath?" he asked, almost offensively.

But the Colonel was unruffled. "It is a prudently lenient government, King William's. I trust it will not press me."

"But if it should?" her ladyship insisted.

"I shall be in a difficulty. I do not know how I shall resolve it."

"You'll know, I suppose, how honour should resolve it for you," said rude Sir Percy.

"With submission, Sir Percy, in what concerns my honour I shall remain the only arbiter."

"Oh, to be sure." Sir Percy was now frankly contemptuous. "Well, I thank God that my opinions are not as yours."

"Quoth the Pharisee," said Colonel Walton, smiling.

Sir Percy glared at him. "Come, my dear," he ordered his wife.

They bowed stiffly, and resumed their walk.

The Colonel put on his hat. He turned to lean once more upon the parapet, his eyes on the placid river in the valley below, his lips pensively smiling.

Invernaion, who had flushed for his friend at the tone Sir Percy took with him, displayed now an angry frown. He waited until the knight and his lady were out of earshot.

"It is not your way, Dudley, to receive insults with such urbanity."

The Colonel's smile grew broader and more enigmatic. "That is because it is not my way to deserve insults."

Invernaion's amazement increased. "Is that a confession that you deserved these?"

"Isn't it plain? Only your friendship for me prevents you from uttering words similar to Sir Percy's. They are in your thoughts."

"But then... If you realize it, Dudley? If you, yourself, perceive what is the only opinion: that what you do is unworthy... Why?"

"I will tell you, Ian. It will explain something else that I have said, but from which you could not extract the kernel of my meaning."

And leaning there upon the parapet, Colonel Walton talked at length, and so persuasively that when he had done Invernaion had not a single argument to advance, a single adverse criticism to offer.

The tale being told, Colonel Walton announced that it was time for him to return to the palace, for the leave-taking audience he had requested of the King. Invernaion linked arms with him as they walked back, and so remained even when they had reached the ante-chamber, and stood under the disapproving glances of those who were already aware of the Colonel's intentions.

Knowing Invernaion's ardour of loyalty, it was supposed by some that he could not yet be informed of the spirit in which the Colonel was departing. One of these ventured to enlighten him, after the Colonel had passed in to his momentous audience. Invernaion's reply astonished all who heard it.

"What then? Dudley Walton is my friend. He remains none the less my friend because his views in this do not happen to be mine."

The Colonel's interview with the King, at which none but Melfort was present, proved a long one. At first this seemed odd to those who marvelled that he should have the audacity to seek an audience at all for the purpose of begging leave to depart to the care of his paltry inheritance. Then it was remembered how high stood the Colonel's reputation as a soldier; that such men were rare in the following of King James, and consequently precious; and that perhaps on this account His Majesty was stifling his pride in an endeavour to persuade him to remain. That opinion persisted among them even after the Colonel had departed at the end of an audience that lasted fully an hour. In his departure, nevertheless, they saw evidence of a hardness of heart which had remained impervious to royal remonstrances.

This widespread assumption was confirmed by one or two contemptuous expressions that Melfort let fall on the subject of Colonel Walton, after his departure.

And such was the suggestion in those words from King James' minister that before the Colonel had reached Calais to embark for England, the members of the Court of Saint Germains had scornfully dismissed so mean a fellow from their minds.

Chapter 11

The Beggar on Horseback

It would be fully twelve months after the discovery and failure of the Assassination Plot, that is to say in the spring of 1697, when after an absence of many years Colonel Dudley Walton made his appearance in London.

By that time the calm that had settled on the life of England was more complete than had been known since William of Orange had landed at Torbay. Never had King William's seat upon the throne been more secure. Never had he been so firmly established in the public esteem.

That there were still in England Jacobites in plenty no one doubted. But it was a thing assumed rather than perceived, for they now hid their diminished heads and kept their politics prudently to themselves.

Colonel Walton, then, seemed fully justified of his desertion of a cause which no longer had any prospects.

His fame as a soldier and the knowledge of his long and close adherence to King James were such that it was impossible that he should be long in London without attracting the attention of the government. Far, however, from seeking to elude this attention, the Colonel actually, and at once, invited it. Immediately upon his arrival he wrote a letter to William Bentinck, Earl of Portland, in which he announced his presence to that diligent minister and friend of King William. He wrote to inform his lordship that he had inherited a small estate in Wiltshire, and that, so that he might come home to administer it, he had resigned a commission which for some years he had held in the French army. He went on to add that since this did not mean that he was content to exchange the sword for the ploughshare, nor that he had reason to suppose that the inheritance would suffice for his needs, however modest, he had the honour humbly to offer his services to King William.

This was a very different story from that which he had told at Saint Germains, where he had announced himself as weary of soldiering, had represented the inherited estate as abundant for his needs, and had expressed the hope that King William's tolerant government would ignore him.

He sat down to wait for an answer, keeping close meanwhile in lodgings which he had taken in Covent Garden, over whose Piazza that Barclay and Invernaion had rendered so famous to Jacobites in the early part of the previous year. He was not kept waiting long before Lord Portland sent for him. He had fully expected this. It was not to be supposed that a communication such as his, from a man such as himself, would be suffered to lie uninvestigated.

In a lofty room of the palace at Kensington sat Portland, to receive him, at a large ormolu-encrusted writing-table with the bowed legs which Dutch influences were introducing into English furniture. The tall windows behind his lordship looked out upon a sweep of emerald lawn to the paler green of burgeoning trees into which the April sunshine brought a touch of gold.

The lean Dutchman, his sallow face, already set in shadow by the fact that the windows were behind him, further obscured by his heavy periwig, took time gravely to ponder his visitor. He had not troubled to rise to receive him, and the nod with which he had acknowledged the suitor's bow was scarcely perceptible.

Colonel Walton understood at once that no courtesies were to be wasted upon him. As he had not been expecting them, he was not put out of countenance. He stood entirely at ease, tall, straight, and very elegant in his burnt-red soldierly coat that was heavy with bullion, set off by the foam of Mechlin lace at throat and wrists.

At the end of his long, searching stare, Portland cleared his throat and spoke. His voice was deep and guttural, proclaiming his origin. His words were hardly encouraging. To Colonel Walton they sorted well with the voice.

"Considering your well-known antecedents," said his lordship, slowly, picking his words with care, "I should scarcely exaggerate if I described your application as impudent."

"You might do so. But you will not," said the Colonel dryly, and set his lordship staring harder than ever.

"Parbleu! And why not?"

"Because you should be wise enough to know the folly of unnecessary offensiveness."

The sallow face was further darkened by a scowl. But the Colonel bore that expression of hostility without departing from his composure. There was, indeed, about him an air of calm that was in itself dominating. Instinctively it must be felt that a man who could so command himself must exercise great power over others. It is possible that my Lord Portland experienced something of this; for gradually the hostility faded from his eyes, and at last these slid away from the soldier's level glance. He uttered a dry little laugh that sounded like a cough.

"Ah, parbleu! You account it offensive for a man in my position to describe the past of a man in yours?"

"I had not remarked that your lordship was about to describe my past. To save you that trouble let me declare at once the worst that is known of me. I have ever been loyal to the hand that paid me."

William Bentinck shrugged. "You have remained abroad until it suits your interest to return to England. Both abroad and at home you have borne arms against His Majesty. It is well known that you were at the Boyne; that you were at Namur; that you were at Steinkirk." He flung out a hand, to point scornfully to the Colonel's loosely knotted lace cravat. "Tenez! You wear the very neck-tie that the Maison du Roi made fashionable there." He smiled sourly, with tight lips. "I am curious – and this is why I have sent for you – to know upon what grounds you can found hopes of being entrusted with a command."

"Your lordship's curiosity is soon gratified. My hopes rest upon my ability as a soldier and your lordship's knowledge of it."

Lord Portland's smile lost nothing of its acidity. "You have a high opinion of yourself, Colonel Walton."

"I reflect the opinion in which I am held by others who are competent to judge. I have here a letter from Monsieur de Villeroy…"

He was carrying his fine hand to the breast of his coat. But his lordship checked the intent, interrupting him. "Let be. Let be. I care nothing for the opinions of Monsieur de Villeroy. Nor do I need them where you are concerned. I know all that Monsieur de Villeroy could tell me. Have you no other basis for these your so extravagant hopes?"

"I could hardly possess any more solid."

"Tenez!" Portland considered him in some surprise. "Ah! Then my curiosity is gratified." He took up a little silver bell and tinkled it. "I shall inform His Majesty of your petition, Colonel Walton. But my advice to you is that you cultivate your acres. It is the only way to make sure that your antecedents will not trouble you."

A servant in the scarlet royal livery made his appearance. Colonel Walton understood. He bowed, ever impassive. If he was disappointed by this dismissal or affronted by the cavalier manner of it, he permitted no shadow to overcast his countenance.

"Your lordship's obliged servant."

He went out briskly, followed, as long as he was in sight, by the dark eyes of the Dutchman, narrowed and speculating.

On the morrow he set out for Wiltshire.

It may have been a natural impatience to survey his heritage that urged him to remove himself so speedily from the capital, or it may have been a prudent desire to avoid the risks of a compromising association with anyone suspected of Jacobite sympathies. The latter explanation is to be preferred, because there is hardly any other that will account for the fact that he should even have neglected to wait upon Lady Lochmore. It might certainly have been expected that he would have sought her, considering the friendship that bound him to her brother, and the fact that he had stood by her late husband in that unfortunate nobleman's inglorious last moments. From nothing so much as from this was it to be argued that Colonel Walton's divorcement from the cause of King James was sincere and absolute.

He took up his residence in the modest country mansion at Avonholme, and let it be known in the county, with a certain emphasis, that he was there. After that he more or less disappears for a season, by which I mean that records are lacking of his activities, and that such scanty knowledge as we actually possess is gleaned retrospectively from meagre particulars transpiring after his re-emergence from country retirement. These, in spite of the exiguity of detail, enable us to construct a fairly complete, if tenuous, chain of events.

It would appear that within a week of establishing himself at Avonholme he gave a house-warming party on a scale that supplied a topic of conversation in Wiltshire for months thereafter. It seems to have been of a prodigality not to be justified by his means or his position in the county, or reconciled with his known habits of sober restraint.

His repute as a soldier and his erstwhile notoriety as a Jacobite combined to render him an interesting figure in all eyes and a romantic one in some. Consequently that house-warming of his was attended by all persons of quality in the county of Wiltshire whom actual distance did not debar from the journey.

Not content with this initial display of munificence, Colonel Walton continued thereafter to dispense at Avonholme a princely hospitality similarly out of all proportion to his position and his estate. On this account, whilst, courtly, suave and gracious, he won the hearts of many, he provoked the sneers of more. His contemners were chiefly the Whigs, who very soon, having satisfied their curiosity, fell away from him. On the other hand, every Tory in the county continued to seek his house and to entertain him in return.

When all is said, there was little in this to excite unfriendly comment. A man of his history could hardly be expected to find his friends in the ranks of the Whigs.

Among the means adopted by county society to dissipate the tedium of existence, high play was prominent. But it is to be doubted if anywhere in Wiltshire play had ever run as high as it did in those days at Avonholme.

Those who had known Colonel Walton abroad might have perceived in this an instance of how a sudden accession of fortune may create such a change in a man's habits as to involve a change in his very nature. For until now cards and the dice-box had found no place in the Colonel's equipment. Having adopted them, however, he seemed unable to keep their use within reasonable bounds.

Before many months had elapsed, the Wiltshire Whigs were justified of their sneering prognostications of what must be the speedy end of this beggar on horseback. The Colonel confessed – to the general surprise, however, of his Tory associates, for fortune had seemed to favour him – that he was so heavy a loser as to be under the necessity of liquidating his estate so that he might clear himself of debt. He received the county's expressions of commiseration with the unruffled suavity and smiling calm which all had come to assume that nothing could disturb.

After all, he opined, the necessity was perhaps a blessing in disguise. His sojourn at Avonholme, whilst in other ways delightful, had abundantly proved to him that his tastes and talents were not agrarian. He supposed that he was too old to change his habits; an assertion which, coming from a man in the early thirties, was received as a jest. Upon the residue of his fortune after the payment of his debts he would take a look at England; and when this residue was spent he would return to France to live once more by his sword like the soldier of fortune that at heart he had remained.

The attractive little estate of Avonholme was readily sold to a neighbouring landowner.

The Colonel paid his debts almost with ostentation, and engagingly frank and open about his concerns, he allowed it be known that he had saved some two thousand guineas from the wreck of his affairs. Bewailed by Wiltshire society, he disappeared from it completely after having so engagingly graced it. If his life as a country squire had been brief, at least it had been splendid.

He appears to have spent the ensuing five or six months upon a sort of grand tour of England, in the course of which he passed from Tory household to Tory household. Again this was no great matter for comment, save that it was a little in the manner of the adventurer. In his present comparatively restricted circumstances it was not surprising that he should seek to take advantage of the hospitality which all good Tories would be prepared to offer a man who in the past had so stoutly served interests akin to their own.

By the following May he was back in London, accompanied only by the French valet, Lavernis, who had come out of France with him.

He occupied again that lodging in Covent Garden, and he moved freely in society, and always in Tory circles. If he should ever be reproached with this he would not be at a loss for a reply, as presently he was to show.

He was much at Gascoigne's, that famous coffee-house by Spring Gardens, which was notoriously a resort of Tories, and here he became acquainted with many who nowadays scarcely made a secret of their Jacobite sympathies. For by now, as Colonel Walton observed, the bolder adherents of King James were at last beginning to recover from the palsy into which they had been cast by the events immediately following the discovery of the Assassination Plot. Unrepressed by a King who dictated lenity as a policy to his government, they began to rear their heads once more and grew insolently careless of where and when they drank to the King Over the Water.

It was at Gascoigne's that Colonel Walton was first presented by Lord Claybourne, whose house he frequented, to James Macdonald, Viscount Glenleven.

The Viscount's manner remained as coldly courteous as was normal with him.

"I have heard of you, sir, from my kinsman, Ian Macdonald of Ivernaion." Instinctively he lowered his voice in uttering the name. Invernaion's fame was of a kind to make a man lower his voice in claiming him for a kinsman.

The Colonel's slow-moving and rather melancholy grey eyes seemed to quicken and harden as they searched the countenance of this slight, elegant gentleman.

"Then you are not likely to have heard anything to my advantage," said he.

Glenleven returned the glance with an eye that was certainly not friendly. "Not of late," he admitted. "But it was not always so. Once, sir, you had no more fervent friend than my cousin Ian. But I am presumptuous. No doubt, Colonel Walton, you are a competent judge of your own actions and of the compensations you will have found for forfeiting so many friendships."

"I endeavour, my lord, to reconcile it with my conscience." The tone was so light, that Glenleven wondered was he mocked.

"You endeavour? That, I think, implies an effort."

"Ha, Colonel," murmured Claybourne, "Glenleven has touched you there."

A large, handsome man this Claybourne, who for all his size was gentle as a woman in his ways. Soft-eyed, soft-voiced, and of a sweet and winning courtesy of manner, he contrasted oddly with the hard brightness of the slight Glenleven.

The Colonel smiled and shrugged without answering, but the smile and the shrug were in themselves eloquent. It was as if he had said: "Perhaps he has. What then?"

Claybourne was encouraged to go further. He turned to Glenleven, bending from his great height.

"Colonel Walton, I think, is a subject for your kinswoman. She will show him the way to make peace with his conscience."

Glenleven's cold eyes were upon the Colonel. "But is that, I wonder, what Colonel Walton wishes? I do not forget that he came to England to offer his sword to King William's government."

"You are well informed, sir," said the Colonel, with an unusual edge to his tone.

Glenleven's brows were raised in surprise. "On a matter of public knowledge? Oh, sir!"

"It is not so public that I should have heard of it," grumbled Claybourne, whose glance had darkened wistfully. "Still, sir, however you may have erred, Lady Lochmore might save your soul for you."

Chapter 12

Colonel Walton Unpacks

Whatever views may have been held by others on the subject of the saving of Colonel Walton's soul, his own view was that he would attend to its salvation in his own fashion.

The immediate step contemplated towards this desirable end was, to the deep thankfulness of his homesick valet Lavernis, once more to cross the Channel, since here in England he discovered now nothing to detain him.

This course undoubtedly he would have followed – in which case I should have had no tale to tell – but for the intervention of Fate in the massive shape of my Lord Claybourne.

That Lancashire Catholic peer was, like most noblemen of his creed, deeply sincere in his loyalty to the exiled Catholic monarch. His most fervent, if at present secret, hopes were founded upon the restoration of King James. It follows that he could not look on indifferently whilst a man of parts so valuable to the cause as those of Colonel Walton remained in the position of neutrality or uncertainty in which he now supposed him to stand.

The intention to bring back this stray lamb to the fold was in his lordship's mind when he contrived that Colonel Walton should be bidden to a rout given by Lady Claybourne.

The Colonel, with all arrangements secretly made for leaving England, suffered himself to be persuaded. He attended the rout on the very eve of his intended departure, and it was here that he made, at last, the acquaintance of Ailsa Lochmore.

Claybourne, himself, presented him, and in doing so began to speak of his qualities. But the young Countess checked him.

"Colonel Walton's name is all the passport he needs here."

The soldier bowed low over the long white hand she proffered. "I was never prouder, ma'am, to bear it than at this moment."

She made a place for him beside her on the settle, and he sank to it gratefully. He told Claybourne later that night that he accounted her more beautiful than any woman that he had ever seen. From her stiff gown of cloth of gold, surmounted by a froth of Valenciennes, arose those shoulders, neck and finely chiselled face that were of the tint of ivory, intensified by the lustrous black of her luxuriant hair. Black too, in the candlelight seemed to him, those liquid dark-blue eyes of hers under the slender black eyebrows.

Ebony and ivory and gold, he pronounced her in his inmost thoughts. She was to him, in her golden gown, like a lovely image wrought by some amazing craftsman, and infinitely more fit for worship.

"What do you in London, Colonel Walton?"

"Until now, madam, I have trifled," said he.

"And now?"

"And now I have seen you."

Gently she moved her fan. Between her eyes a frown appeared. But her lips smiled. "I am a gorgon, then, that the sight of me should change a man?"

He shook his head. "You do not change him into stone."

"Faith, sir, you are almost as placid."

"The placidity of deep waters, ma'am."

"Pray do not drown me in them, or in the subtlety of your flattery. Shall we be serious, sir? Do you think the time is one in which Colonel Walton should be trifling?"

"I have said, madam, that that is ended."

Her dark eyes were intently studying him over the edge of her fan, which screened now the lower half of her face. "But you leave me in doubt of your true meaning."

"I dare do no more whilst standing thus upon the threshold of acquaintance."

"You may enter, and improve it. At my house you will meet old friends."

"By your ladyship's gracious leave, I shall come in the hope of making a new one."

Again she frowned a little whilst she continued to search his baffling countenance. "You will regard me as that?"

"I have some small claim to do so. Your brother honoured me with his friendship."

"I know. I know."

"And your husband died in my arms."

"Ah, yes. I remember that, too." She looked him squarely in the face, with a frank directness. "It is as if Fate had somehow already linked us."

"It is not often that Fate has dealt so kindly by me."

Yet again the frown appeared between the eyes, and this time there was no smile upon the lips to mitigate it. "You said that you had done with trifling."

"Must I repeat it before you will believe me?"

"I should prefer that you give proof of it. In spite of the claims you have discerned to my acquaintance, you have been at no pains to establish them. Yet you have been some time in England."

"Something over a year," he said, confining his reply to that.

"You came from France. From Saint Germains."

He inclined his head in silent assent.

"And you were with His Majesty? He does not lose heart I hope."

He took time to answer her. When at last he did so, he lowered his voice. "I speak, of course, from the standpoint of a year ago when I say that his hopes are higher than their justification here in England."

He saw the dark liquid eyes dilate as if with pain. He had startled her.

"How can you say that?" There was sharp repudiation in her tone.

"I speak as I have found."

"You have not known where to look."

He smiled gently in silence, and then felt her hand cool upon his wrist, and quivered at the touch of her. "Let me help you."

"I could conceive," said he very solemnly, "no greater happiness."

"You choose to be oracularly ambiguous. But I will not suppose your meaning to be personal to myself."

Because her tone held a reproof he made haste to satisfy her doubt.

"That were an audacity of which I could not yet be guilty."

"Not yet?" She raised her brows again. Then she laughed, and her countenance cleared. "You relieve me at least in part. Seek me soon, Colonel Walton, and I will prove to you that things in England are not as somnolent as the surface may have led you to fear."

"Did I say 'fear,' madam?"

"If you did not say it, I must hope that it was in your mind."

Much later he was to tell Invernaion how her deep, almost tragic earnestness had filled him with a vague alarm, which remained unaccountable until later reflection made him realize its nature. It was impossible to mistake her meaning or the object of the invitation she extended.

Whilst Invernaion welcomed his sister's secret and very useful co-operation, yet, as we know, he had ever been at pains to keep her out of all enterprises by which she might come to be compromised. So far had he carried this that not in his most intimate moments had he given Colonel Walton a hint which might have prepared him for the state of things her words disclosed. Not only did she more than imply the existence of Jacobite activity, but she made it plain that she was deep in whatever plot was being hatched. The little that she had said sufficed to clear up the obscurity of Lord Claybourne's assertion that Lady Lochmore might save the Colonel's soul for him.

Now Dudley Walton was instinctively fearful of plots in which women were included. Yet here his alarm was of quite another kind. It was personal. Its roots were in concern for this lady, so young, so lovely, and so desirable in body and in mind, this lady whom yesterday he had not known, but who, nevertheless, was the sister of his friend.

Was it possible that Invernaion could be aware of the activities in which her ladyship was engaged, activities which, despite the government's lenity, had never in Colonel Walton's view been more dangerous than they now were? He had been prepared, of course, to find her sympathies frankly Jacobite. No man was more fully aware than he of the justification which the Macdonalds believed they possessed for this. But he was far from prepared to find her, as her words all but avowed, concerned in some business whose aim was the subversion of the existing government. So appalled was he that he was actually considering the framing of some warning, of some remonstrance, when he grew conscious that they were being observed.

Across the room he met the watching eyes of Major O'Grady, an associate of Claybourne's and Glenleven's, whose acquaintance the Colonel had made at Gascoigne's, and of whom all that he knew was that the man had fought for King James and had been severely wounded in the second siege of Limerick, and that he was now living quietly in London, ignored by a government which did not believe in making martyrs.

The observer, upon perceiving that he was, himself, observed, advanced at once, a tall, spare man with a nut-cracker face, an ugly, curving mouth, and dark, close-set eyes.

"Gracious lady, your fervent worshipper." He bowed over the hand which with friendly readiness she extended. "Colonel Walton, your humble obedient."

The Colonel was frigid. Major O'Grady's intrusion could not have been more untimely. Yet, having joined them, the Irishman lingered, insensible to the Colonel's frigidity, which so plainly invited him to depart again.

With what patience he could command the Colonel waited for the opportunity to probe this matter further, as he was urged to do both out of his affection for Invernaion and out of the interest which Invernaion's sister, herself, aroused in him. He was reduced to despair when presently Lady Claybourne came irresistibly to bear him off.

Those who subsequently met him that evening accounted him taciturn and dull.

He was still lost in the thoughts accountable for this when he reached home at midnight. There he was greeted by the soft-footed, quiet-mannered Lavernis with the assurance that all their packages were made, and that in the morning they could go aboard the cutter that waited at Blackwall.

"You can unpack again, Lavernis."

"Comment?" Lavernis was horrified. "We do not, then, depart?"

"Not yet, tomorrow," said the Colonel.

The valet sighed dolefully. His first thought was for himself. "Now that is a thing that is sad." His second thought was for his master. Instinctively he lowered his voice. "Is Monsieur le Colonel prudent to remain?"

"Damned imprudent, Lavernis. Nevertheless, departure is for the moment postponed. The cutter can wait. We are not at war, now, and Dubois' papers are in order. I'll resolve in a day or two."

Chapter 13

The Tempter

Colonel Walton kept his lodging until the evening of the morrow.

The dejected Lavernis, furtively observing him, was concerned to the point of alarm by his master's gloomy pensiveness.

When at last the Colonel went forth at dusk, it was to take his way to Gascoigne's. It is to be suspected that he was deliberately putting himself in the way of those whom he judged to be Lady Lochmore's associates in treason. At Gascoigne's he found Glenleven in the company of Major O'Grady, who of late had become as close and constant as a shadow in his attendance upon the Viscount. He found there also another acquaintance in that notorious gamester, Sir Anthony Cliffe, who, lacking at the moment an opponent, hailed him effusively.

Consistent with the reputation he had earned, he yielded to the newly conceived passion for play, which, as all the world knew by now, was supposed to have lost him his Wiltshire estate. He sat down to hazard with Sir Anthony, and rose at four o'clock in the morning the poorer by some two hundred guineas.

Sir Anthony would still have continued the game on the pretext of affording the Colonel an opportunity of retrieving his losses. But the Colonel, stifling a yawn behind his fine hand, objected coolly that the loss of necessary sleep would hardly compensate him for the recovery of his guineas.

O'Grady, who with Glenleven had lingered, and who had now for some time been watching the game, drew his lordship aside, and held him closely in muttered talk whilst the Colonel was settling accounts with Sir Anthony. This was something that the Colonel was later to remember, as also that whenever he had turned his eyes in their direction, he had found their glances furtively upon him, as if he were supplying the subject of their talk.

On the threshold, in the pearly dawn, the soldier found Glenleven at his elbow.

"Will you walk, Colonel? Our ways lie together for some distance."

Something indefinable in that musical voice made the Colonel suspect the purpose behind his lordship's proposal. For this reason, rather than because the invitation was not one that without offence he could have refused, he readily assented.

They set out, and walked some little way towards Charing Cross in a silence that was odd. Colonel Walton did not choose to break it. Deliberately he waited for his companion to fulfil the purpose which he supposed him to have in mind. If Glenleven also preserved silence it was, the Colonel surmised, because he was finding a difficulty in discovering a starting point for what he had to say. At last, however, he let fall an observation.

"Do not take it amiss if I commend the spirit in which you bear your losses, Colonel."

"It honours me that your lordship should commend anything of mine." Colonel Walton spoke in that dry tone that often left men wondering whether he laughed at them when he was most pleasant.

If his lordship was troubled by any such doubt he put it aside.

"I rate a good loser highly, because the man who knows how to lose without repining, will always prove the winner in the end, no matter what the game."

"It is evident, then, that I have not yet reached the end," said the Colonel in the same dry voice. It was no part of his intent to further his lordship's purpose; a purpose towards which he rightly sensed that these generalities were mere preambles.

"Yet you may be nearer to it than you suppose."

"Perhaps I may. They say in Italy that all ills are not sent to harm us. My losses at play drive me back to find employment for my sword, which, after all, is the fittest employment for a gentleman."

Here was the opening for which Glenleven played. Into it he flashed his retort. "Provided the sword is worthily employed." And without pause he added the question: "You have employment for it?"

The Colonel smiled. The question was ingenuous. "Your lordship knows where it was last offered."

"Oh yes. But that was a year ago. That is in the past. My concern is for your future."

"The concern flatters me. I can return to French service, since in England no service offers, and King William's government looks askance on me."

"And have you, sir, cause to look otherwise upon King William?"

The Colonel shrugged. "When I became an English landowner, expediency suggested that I should make my peace." And then, almost by way of apology, as it seemed, he added: "After all, my lord, you are to remember that I am a soldier first and last. A soldier of fortune, you might call me. I should not take offence at the appellation."

Glenleven made him no reply. The Colonel's words appeared to have sunk his lordship into thought. In silence they paced on until they had come by the cross of Queen Eleanor into the Strand, and there met a patrol of the watch, whose lanterns gleamed as ineffectually yellow as painted lights in the increasing daylight.

The constable surveyed them, and gave them good morrow respectfully, since their cloaks and laced hats announced a quality to command respect.

Presently, when they had walked a little way farther, his lordship fulfilled the Colonel's expectations by returning to the attack.

"And so, the members of King William's government look askance on you?"

"I do not blame them."

"And they have ignored your applications."

"I am neither surprised nor plaintive."

"Ah! Not even when this indifference to your undoubted talents drives you to seek employment overseas?"

The Colonel shrugged again. "What profit lies in repining?"

Glenleven was almost impatient. "Sir, you would have me suppose that you enjoy being ruined."

They had walked some little way before the Colonel answered him. "What is your lordship's interest to thwart me in my self-deception?"

"The interest, sir, to serve you, if you will be served."

"To serve me!" Colonel Walton's voice rose in surprise. He checked in his stride. Glenleven halted with him, and they stood in the middle of the street, facing each other. "How, my lord, have I deserved your favour?"

"By your antecedents. You were once in the service of King James, and like so many others you followed him to France. Whilst you awaited his call, you entered French service because France was sheltering him. That makes you a Jacobite. You'll not trouble to deny it."

"Your lordship goes too fast and perhaps too far. Nor is my history quite as you suppose it. It is true that I was at the Boyne. But, when all is said, I am neither a Scot nor a Papist. As I have told you, sir, and as I told my Lord of Portland, I am a soldier of fortune, and I serve the hand that pays."

"Why, then, since you put it no higher, it might be mine to show you where the best pay awaits you."

They were moving on again by now. "I suspect, my lord, that you are proposing to talk treason."

"On a privileged occasion, and to a man of honour. Besides, what is treason? Is it treason to invite you to serve your lawful King against a foreign usurper? Those who serve a King in his need are those who prosper when the King comes into his own again. Thus, Colonel Walton, duty and profit go hand in hand for you."

"A comfortable condition. It is such that might suit me, I confess. What is involved, my lord?"

The direct question left his lordship thoughtful for some moments. "Come with me one day soon to my Lady Lochmore's, and you shall learn."

"I should prefer," said the Colonel, "to know before I go. What is the plot you hatch there, my lord?"

"Plot?" His lordship was startled. "Did I speak of a plot?"

"You did not use the word. But I am not a child; and even a child could assume nothing else." And again, almost sternly, almost as if with authority, the soldier asked: "What is the nature of this plot? Its aim?"

It was Glenleven's turn to halt and face his companion. Save for themselves the street was utterly empty, although it was now broad daylight.

"Are you with us?" his lordship demanded. "Are you, or are you not?"

"That is an odd question to set a man before informing him of what's to do."

The Viscount's narrow young face became a mask. But his blue eyes were hard and stern. "You have reminded me, sir, that you are not a child. You know more than enough upon which to make your decision. The rest you shall learn when the decision is made."

The Colonel fingered his lip, considering. "If you will come... " he was slowly beginning, and there broke off, like a man who changes his mind. Abruptly, "Let me sleep on it, my lord," he said.

"With all my heart. I could not wish you to enter upon such a matter until after full consideration. If you decide that you are with us, seek me again at Gascoigne's." And abruptly his lordship loosened his cloak and held out his hand in leave-taking.

Chapter 14

Employment

Apparently sleep brought the Colonel no counsel. For at noon on the morrow when he sat up in bed over the chocolate which his servant brought him, he had only misgivings to express.

"To pack, or not to pack, Lavernis. That is the question. If I distress you longer by continuing in this cold afflicted land of fogs which it seems you can never learn to love, I am likely myself to be distressed. My Lord Argus of Portland's many eyes will be suspiciously upon me now that I am seen to have no honest reason for remaining; now that according to the appearances, necessity, that most peremptory of mistresses, should be driving me away.

"What view do you take of all this, Lavernis?"

The sleek young valet inclined himself a little.

"Dubois waits at Blackwall with the cutter, my colonel."

"That is an answer. Yes. But you are an egotist, Lavernis. You reply out of your own desires, instead of out of my necessities. Dubois shall continue to wait, even as I must, until I can resolve myself. And my Lord of Portland's many eyes must be dusted. The stage is set. The corroborative evidence is already provided. Behold me a ruined man, Lavernis. Bring me my bed-gown, pen, ink and paper."

So the Colonel wrote once more to King William's friend and minister, to solicit employment, and he couched his letter in most urgent terms.

He confessed that the modest fortune inherited a year ago had been entirely dissipated; that between himself and want stood little more than the means to pay his journey back to France, where his long sojourn in England might bring him now under suspicion and exclude him from a return to the service which he had quitted.

Thus his lingering in England would, he conceived, be satisfactorily explained to Portland. His lordship must assume him so foolish as to continue in hopes of being employed by the government of King William, and detained by nothing more than this hope.

The result of his letter, however, exceeded by far all that Colonel Walton was expecting.

Having kept his lodgings for two days, dreaming troubled dreams about the lady of ivory and ebony and gold, but without apparently coming to any definite resolve, he was startled on the morning of Monday by a curt note commanding him to wait again upon my Lord Portland.

Within a couple of hours of the receipt of that command, you see Colonel Walton once more closeted with his lordship in that handsome room in the Palace at Kensington. Again, as a year ago, the Dutchman sat at the ormolu-encrusted writing-table, with his back to the light from the tall windows. Again the Colonel stood straight and tall and very elegant, in blue velvet this time, with that same light full upon his vigorously handsome, uncannily calm features.

So much as he could discern of Portland's countenance was forbidding. His lordship's eyes considered him at length before breaking the silence. Then, when at last his harsh, guttural voice was heard in the fluent and rather precise English that he employed, his opening expressions were far from promising.

"In the time that you have spent in England," said his lordship, "you have added to what was formerly known of you nothing that might commend you to His Majesty."

"One thing, I think," said the imperturbable Colonel. "Necessity."

"There is a proverb to the effect that it knows no laws."

"Save those which are imposed upon it. The proverb-maker should have added that."

"I do not think I understand."

"Then I'll add another proverb that will perhaps explain. 'Beggars may not be choosers'."

"I do not perceive the elucidation. I am dull, perhaps."

"I mean, my lord, that the necessity which drives me so pertinaciously to seek the King's service will compel me to study zealously to retain it. In some sort that is a guarantee of good faith."

"If so, it is the only one you have yet supplied."

"At least, I trust, I have not had the misfortune to supply any to the contrary."

"Have you not, sir? Have you not? Ah, parbleu! Do you conceive His Majesty's government to be blind? Do you imagine, sir, that we know nothing of your activities in this past year?"

"Activities!" The Colonel smiled. "It is the last word I should apply to the idle drifting in which I have consumed a modest fortune."

"So! So! Yes. But whither have you drifted? From one Jacobite household to another. A man herds by instinct with his kind. Is it not?"

"If your lordship will substitute Tory for Jacobite, I'll accept the impeachment. But as for Jacobites – faith! – I found none in my wanderings."

"Were you looking for them?" flashed Portland, like a swordsman whirling his point into a sudden opening. And as he spoke, he leaned forward sharply to observe the effect of his thrust.

It was parried by a melancholy smile. "If I had been, I must now have every reason to conclude that the cause of King James lies under a blight in the country."

Portland sank back again in his tall chair. His eyes were veiled by lowered lids. "Is that the conclusion that brings you back here to seek employment at the hands of King William?"

"I protest your lordship is not very generous."

"You lay claim to my generosity? That is amusing."

"Since your lordship's assumption appears to agree with my own that there are no Jacobites left in England, it must follow that I cannot have consorted with any."

"Parbleu! You reason like an attorney. But you'll not dispel facts by a cheap illusion of logic. I say to you plainly that you have not been discreet in your associations; that your conduct inspires no confidence."

Now it would have been plain to wits much duller than those of Colonel Walton that the Earl of Portland had not commanded him to Kensington just to tell him this. It followed that there must be some purpose behind it, and one which the minister was approaching tortuously. The Colonel became vaguely uneasy. But he kept to the matter.

"Do you blame me, my lord, for accepting the only hospitality that was offered to me? Your lordship knows how vainly I should have sought admission to the households of the Whigs."

Bentinck's glance became charged with scorn. It sounded, too, in his voice. "You commend yourself vastly, by my faith! You confess yourself a broken gamester. You confess to sponging upon men's hospitality. You are not concerned to avoid contempt, Monsieur l'escroc."

Beyond a darkening of colour in the Colonel's face, its calm remained.

"It is not every man who is in your lordship's fortunate position of being able to manifest it with impunity. I console myself with that reflection."

"Ah, bah! Let us keep to the business."

"It would be more amiable, my lord."

"Leave we the country. Come we now to town. I find you consorting here with such men as my Lord Glenleven, my Lord Claybourne, Harry Dalkeith, and many more of the kind. Will you pretend to ignorance that these men are avowed Jacobites? Will you describe them as merely Tories? You have dined more than once at Dalkeith's with men of his own traitorous kidney. You were at a rout at my Lady Claybourne's, some few nights ago, where every man and most of the women are of those who daily toast the King Over the Water."

The Colonel answered in a tone of mild surprise, "If your lordship is so well informed of their treason, why do you suffer them at large?"

His lordship bridled. He smote the table irritably with his open hand.

"Sirrah, you are not here to set me questions; but to answer mine. I am waiting."

"I heard no question. But I will infer it. My answer is the same as before. Until His Majesty's government accredits me with employment I can find no friend save those of Tory sympathies."

"Tory sympathies! I thought we should have that euphemism. And therefore you sit in long and intimate talk with that Jacobite firebrand, Lady Lochmore."

To the Colonel this was a blow between the eyes. He quivered where he stood. He was conscious of cold along his spine, and for a fraction of time was almost shaken out of his imperturbable demeanour. But he made an instantaneous recovery. He inclined his head a little. A deprecatory little smile took shape upon his lips.

"Her ladyship is a very beautiful woman."

Portland sneered at him audibly. "You answer everything, do you not? Well, well! I have yet another question for you. Let me hear you answer that. What proposals has my Lord Glenleven made to you? You are not so ready, eh? You stare?"

The Colonel stared, indeed. But only for a moment. At the end of it, his melancholy, wistful smile appeared. "It took me by surprise a little that your lordship should resort to the hoary trick of pretending knowledge so as to entrap admissions."

"Pretending! I pretend? I?" Portland betrayed heat. A flush glowed through the sallow surface of his lean, bony face. "If I were to tell you… " he began, and abruptly checked, like a man who suddenly perceives that he is about to say too much.

The Colonel's impassivity never allowed his lordship to suspect that he had said too much already.

He resumed more smoothly: "Will you deny that you were bidden by Glenleven to Lady Lochmore's?"

"But why should I deny it?"

"So. Did you accept the invitation?"

"No, my lord."

"No? Did you refuse it?"

"I was vague, my lord. Her ladyship, as I have had the honour to mention, is a very beautiful woman. I do not easily resist the invitations of a beautiful woman. I was tempted."

The sallow countenance before him became utterly inscrutable. A silence followed and for some moments the only sound in that spacious, lofty room was the ticking of the Dutch clock upon the overmantel.

Then, at last, the Earl of Portland spoke. In an odd voice, pregnant with significance, he said slowly: "You may yield to that temptation, Colonel Walton, in the service of His Majesty."

The words being spoken, the silence was resumed and continued for a spell. The Colonel was frowning. "I hardly apprehend," he said at last.

Watching him keenly, an acid smile on his lips, Portland explained himself.

"Necessity makes you importunate for employment. You have reminded me that beggars cannot be choosers. So that you have employment, then, you will be indifferent to its nature?"

"Provided that it is honourable employment."

"In the King's service, sir, there is no other."

"Ah! And yet I seem to have heard of the common hangman."

Lord Portland clucked irritably. "I have said that you answer everything. You talk too much. You are pert and tiresome. Let us come straight to the matter, and have done. No need for many words.

"At Lady Lochmore's, when you go there, you will find yourself in a nest of treason in which another assassination plot is being hatched. I can supply you with the names of all the plotters you will meet there, and of one whom you will not meet.

"This one is Ian Macdonald of Invernaion, Lady Lochmore's brother. He keeps prudently abroad; and even there, of late, he has a trick of disappearing; he is as elusive as he is dangerous; and in this plot he is at once the brain to conceive and the arm to execute.

"It will be best that I am entirely frank with you, so that you will understand.

"If I do not put my foot at once upon this wasp's nest, it is because to do so would be to warn this knave Macdonald. And so," he added very slowly, "the only one of them who really matters to me would escape, to begin again as soon as opportunity serves. And I do not mean him to escape. I do not intend that my rest shall be forever disturbed and my mind constantly preoccupied by this rogue's desperate activities. J'en ai assez! I mean to make an end of him. The other plotting fools... Pish! They are nothing. Invernaion, that is a man to fear, I confess it; a man who already has given us incalculable trouble and done incalculable harm; a bold, resolute, enterprising villain. But there! Let me but have word, definite word, of this Invernaion's whereabouts, and, wherever he may be, my agents shall find him for me."

He paused there, and his eyes which whilst he had been speaking had never for a moment left the Colonel's face, seemed to grow yet more fixed in their regard. "Sooner or later this so precious information must be obtainable at Lady Lochmore's."

So! The murder was out at last, and the reason why he had been summoned to the Palace was at last clear to the Colonel. Under his icy front a volcano of indignation was raging. For the sake of his self-respect he must affect, he felt, not yet to understand that anyone should dare to insult him by such a proposal.

"If all is as your lordship is informed, that would seem to follow. But how does it concern me?"

"Are you dull? Or do you pretend to be? At the hands of her ladyship a welcome awaits you. Are you not a distinguished soldier, esteemed of Monsieur de Villeroy, and of proven loyalty in the past to King James? And are you not, therefore, of value in the councils of these traitors, and no doubt in the actions that are to follow out of them?

"You will accept the invitation you have received. You will procure me this information. You will also discover for me in what circumstances, on what occasion, the blow they intend is to be struck.

"I will have you take no risk of failure. Therefore, you will not attempt to communicate with me, until you can bring me the complete information I require."

The Colonel stood like a statue. Lord Portland's dark eyes searching that lofty countenance on which the light beat fully, found it of a masklike impassivity. The voice, when presently it came, was toneless.

"This is the service your lordship offers to a gentleman?"

"It is the service I offer to a man whose antecedents make it necessary that he should be tested. That I offer it at all, is already a proof of goodwill. If you succeed in this task, and thus prove yourself, be sure that employment better suited to your acknowledged talents will await you. And in the meantime it is work that will be well recompensed. His Majesty's government has raised to five thousand pounds the reward it is now offering for information that will lead to the arrest of Ian Macdonald."

"My lord, this is unworthy."

"Unworthy?" The dark brows arched themselves. "Peste! Unworthy a broken gamester who confesses himself an escroc? Tiens!"

"Oh, a broken gamester, if you please; and an escroc as well, to put it brutally. But a spy... A spy upon those who are to take me trustingly into their confidence! A Judas to entrap and betray to you a man, so that you may deliver him to the hangman! That is too much, my lord, even for a broken gamester and an escroc."

Portland drummed with his fingers impatiently upon the polished surface of his table.

"You boggle at a word. What need to call yourself by an ugly name? You will be an agent of the government, working to avoid a national calamity and to thwart an assassin. Is that dishonourable?"

"Descriptions do not change the nature of things."

Bentinck shrugged. "Bien! A pity you so regard it. You decline, then?"

Had the question come three heartbeats earlier, the answer would have been prompt. But in that fraction of time, even whilst his lordship had been speaking, the Colonel had caught a fleeting glimpse of something that showed itself elusive and fugitive on the horizon of his mind. Because of this he now stood silent, his square chin buried in his fine cravat, a man considering; and considering infinitely more than the astute Dutchman who observed him even began to suspect. His mind was galloping through an analysis of the knowledge of which Lord Portland had shown himself possessed.

To obtain this knowledge, Colonel Walton's travels through England need not have been followed step by step by government spies. From odd scraps of information upon the course of those travels the rest might easily have been inferred.

Knowledge of his presence at Lady Claybourne's rout was readily explained. No doubt Portland had been supplied with a list of the guests at that assembly in the house of so suspect a person. The Colonel's close talk with Lady Lochmore would not have wanted for observers. Even as the thought occurred to him, he had a fleeting mental vision of the dark nut-cracker face of Major O'Grady so intently watching them. What O'Grady had seen would have been seen by others.

Nothing mysterious so far.

Even Lord Portland's acquaintance with the business that brought that bunch of plotters together at Lady Lochmore's was not beyond explanation. These Jacobites living under a government which was tolerant from policy, because it did not believe in making martyrs, were emboldened to push indiscretion to the point of recklessness. Lady Claybourne's rout had been an instance of this. Government agents quietly listening – men perhaps as much above suspicion as himself, and similarly enlisted – would pick up scraps here and there, which when assembled might make up a fairly complete tale.

But Portland's knowledge of Glenleven's unwitnessed talk with Colonel Walton on that early morning walk from Gascoigne's was in another class altogether. It must remain fraught with mystery unless to be explained by the assumption that Portland, informed that they had left Gascoigne's together in the hours of daybreak, had drawn a bow at a venture on the subject of the uses Glenleven might have made of such an opportunity.

There was, however, no assumption discernible to him that would explain the deeper mystery of Lord Portland's motives for entrusting this particular piece of espionage to Colonel Walton.

His lordship pretended that it was to be a test of loyalty. That, however, was to reverse the logical order of things. The task was one that could be entrusted only to a man whose loyalty was already firmly established. The Colonel's antecedents, as Portland rightly said, inspired no confidence. What assurance could Portland possess that Colonel Walton would not employ the knowledge gained so as to warn the plotters and disperse them? Was that the aim? To employ him as a sort of scarecrow? It might be. But the explanation did not satisfy him, because he knew, of his own knowledge, that Portland by no means overstated the case when he represented the suppression of Invernaion as urgently necessary to his peace of mind.

Was this shrewd Dutchman really acting upon the conviction that a man who did not deny that he was a broken gamester and an escroc, would, upon being faced with dire necessity, desperately stifle the last scruple? That to a man in his case the temptation to earn five thousand pounds with an assurance of honourable employment to follow must prove irresistible? Did Portland really regard Colonel Walton as a drowning man who would clutch at any straw, no matter how dirty?

It was possible. Consequently, considering how singularly adapted was the Colonel's history to win him the confidence of Lady

Lochmore's circle, Lord Portland might well regard him as a tool so opportune to his needs as to be employed even at some risk.

After all, where else should Portland find a man in Colonel Walton's circumstances, for whom a welcome was assured in that assembly of plotters?

Where else?

And then, promptly, in answer to this question, came a suspicion that turned him cold. Was it possible that such an agent had been found already, and could this be the explanation of Portland's intimate acquaintance with the plot?

For an instant Colonel Walton thought that he had resolved the problem, only to perceive in the next how absurd was the solution. In such a case Lord Portland would certainly not now be requiring Colonel Walton, or disposed to make the gambler's throw which employing him entailed.

Thus far into that queer maze had his thoughts travelled when his lordship's voice came harshly to recall him to the decision to be made.

"Well, sir? Well? Do you decline, or do you accept?"

Colonel Walton emerged from his absorption. Expression dawned on his blank countenance. Slowly, his features relaxed into a deprecating smile. At last, he gave a little shrug with an air of recklessness.

"As your lordship so wisely perceives, a man in my circumstances cannot afford a high stomach. I will not pretend to eagerness. I will not… Oh! But there! What use are words? I accept the task, my lord, as an earnest of better things to follow."

His lordship continued to ponder him searchingly. At length, as if satisfied, he spoke, and his tone was less harsh.

"Serve the King diligently in this, Colonel Walton, and be sure that better things will follow. Your military talents shall be given scope. Fail me, play me false in the least degree, and be equally sure that you will have destroyed yourself. I have a long arm, Colonel Walton, as I count upon you to enable me to demonstrate to Macdonald of Invernaion. You will have perceived, I think, from what I have told you, that His Majesty's government is well equipped with eyes."

Colonel Walton had, indeed, perceived it. It was this perception, the very thing that it might be supposed would have deterred him, which had – although Lord Portland, for all his shrewdness was far from suspecting it – been the force that had urged him into this contemptible undertaking.

Chapter 15

The Plot

To Lochmore House, Lady Lochmore's small mansion in the Strand, came Colonel Walton to dine on a day of that week which had opened with his interview with the Earl of Portland.

He was conducted by my Lord Glenleven, to whose proposals he had hastened immediately to return the answer which the government service rendered necessary.

He was very graciously welcomed by his lovely hostess, and received with manifest warmth by the company. This was made up entirely of men; the handsome, portly Lord Claybourne; young Sir Hamish Stuart of Meorach, tall, plump, florid, and frog-eyed; little Geoffrey Howard, pallid and effete; long, fair, willowy Harry Dalkeith; and the saturnine Major O'Grady.

When the cloth had been raised, the comfits and sweet wines were circulating, and the servants had withdrawn, her ladyship rapped the table to impose silence, and then stood before them with the solemnity of a priestess. She rose to give them the toast of the King.

Which King she meant was made plain by the ritual that accompanied her words. With a sweeping, dramatic gesture, she brought her glass over a silver bowl of water on which some lilies floated, and held it so whilst she pledged His Majesty.

The company, as solemnly responsive, came to its feet. Eight wine-glasses met in a cluster above that same bowl; and in unison came the cry: "The King!"

The Colonel, as the guest of honour on her ladyship's immediate right, bore his part in this mummery, no trace of the scornful humour with which he witnessed it, reflected on his face.

When it was over, and they had resumed their seats, Lord Claybourne came abruptly to business, earnestly addressing their latest recruit. His lordship understood that the Colonel held certain definite views on affairs in France and on the attitude towards England of King Louis, and he invited him to communicate them freely to the company.

In expectant silence the company's eyes were turned upon the Colonel. He did not strain the expectancy.

"You will remember," he said slowly, "that for the past year I have been in England."

"Lotus-eating," her ladyship reproved him, tapping his knuckles with her fan.

He acknowledged the reproof by a smile, but did not directly answer it at the moment.

"When I left France there was certainly no lukewarmness on the part of King Louis in the matter of lending his support to the cause of King James."

"Ay!" interjected the croaking voice of O'Grady. "The orange is not a fruit they cultivate in France. But ye'll not be implying, now, that King Louis may have changed since then?"

"Alas! No."

That set them staring at him.

"Do you say 'alas'?" cried her ladyship.

"You'll give me reason when you have heard me. King Louis' sympathies are fixed. Any change, therefore, must have been from sympathy to action. It is of this that I perceive no sign or chance."

"No chance?" said Dalkeith, impatiently. And then Stuart of Meorach took up the argument. He was glib of speech and forceful of manner.

"How can you venture to assert so much? With what authority can you speak to what may have happened in the year of your absence from France?"

"With the authority, Sir Hamish, of what I find in England." The Colonel turned his calm grey eyes upon her ladyship. "Oh, I have not entirely been lotus-eating, although I have allowed it to be supposed. In my travels through the country I have been observing; observing closely."

"And you have found?" she asked him, her white face eager.

"A deadlock. Here is the situation, as I should by now have reported it at Saint Germains if my departure had not been postponed by the representations of my Lord Glenleven and his invitation to join you. The country will rise if King Louis sends an army."

"Ah!" ejaculated Claybourne.

And the others were all suddenly leaning forward, their eager glances on the Colonel's face.

The Colonel continued.

"But King Louis will send an army only if the country rises. Each waits upon the other. Neither will hazard the first move. From this stalemate I perceive no issue."

Their eagerness perished in disappointment. But from this her ladyship was quick to rally.

"We may be able to supply one," she said, and an emphatically assenting murmur supported the assertion.

Colonel Walton looked round the table, an obvious question in his glance. Sir Hamish answered it.

"If the deadlock is as bad as your pessimism supposes, it can endure only while William of Orange lives. Once he's out of the way, that deadlock is broken. There will not then even be the need for troops from France."

"Very true," the Colonel agreed. "But, meanwhile, King William's health whilst not of the best is far from affording grounds for your hopes. Asthmatical men often contrive to live on."

They looked at one another with significance, yet with doubt and question in their glances. Then her ladyship, with a gesture as of brushing something aside, urged frankness. The Colonel, she protested, was entirely to be trusted. Despite a certain lukewarmness for a season, dictated by personal policy, he had just made it clear that he had never wavered in his sympathy towards a King whom he had so signally served. The fact that he was now amongst them, the intention he had disclosed of returning to Saint Germains to make his report and all his past record supplied the completest guarantees of his loyalty.

That confident assurance made an end of reticences. The existence of a plot well advanced in the hatching, and the full aim of it, were now revealed to him, precisely as the well-informed Lord Portland had revealed it to him already.

William of Orange was to be killed.

In addition he was informed by Stuart of Meorach – and it was obviously news also to one or two others among those present – that the occasion would be supplied when William presently went over to the Hague to open the States, a matter which he must perform before the end of the month.

Thus, at the very outset, Colonel Walton became possessed of one of the facts which Portland desired to ascertain.

To this her ladyship added, speaking with obvious pride in her brother, that Invernaion was ready. He but awaited the signal, which would be given him by those now present at this board. Their own chief function was to ascertain and communicate to him the precise date of William's journey.

The Colonel listened with a countenance from which he did not trouble to dissemble gravity. By the time their explanations came to an end his expression was forbidding.

"But this," he said slowly, like a man appalled, "is murder. Murder!"

For a moment his word and tone seemed to knock the breath out of them all. Her ladyship, beside him, at the table's head, shrank into her tall chair, as if away from him, staring at him the while with startled eyes.

Then from one or two came half-angry interjections. O'Grady laughed his harsh laugh in fierce derision, but said nothing. It was Lord Claybourne at last, his handsome countenance preserving its gentle air, who leaned across the board to reason in mildest accents with the Colonel.

"If King James were to return at the head of an army and were to prevail, would not the life of the Prince of Orange be forfeit for his usurpation? In the battles that would follow the King's landing, thousands of men might come to perish. Could that be called murder? We – too small a group to deliver battle to an army – must snatch our victory by aiming directly at the battle's ultimate object."

Stuart of Meorach took up the argument with greater heat.

"Wherein lies the difference between the two operations? If there is any, it is that we prevail by gentler means. We avert an ocean of bloodshed. We sacrifice one life only so as to accomplish that for which every loyal heart must pray. And we take the view that what we do is an act of war. Upon what sane grounds are we to be gainsaid? Is it to be pretended that the difference between war and murder lies in the number of the slain? Is murder to become dignified by the name of war simply because there are a thousand dead instead of one? Is that what you would say, Colonel Walton?"

The Colonel's gesture, almost contemptuous, brushed aside the arguments.

"These are the usual hoary sophistries of regicides. Words, sirs, cannot change the nature of a deed."

Her ladyship leaned towards him again. "No. But they can bring us to a proper vision of what that nature is. Murder, Colonel, is a killing done for personal, selfish ends. This is a killing for the general good, and to the end that right may triumph over wrong, and triumph, as my Lord Claybourne has said, without the unnecessary shedding of innocent blood. Can you deny the truth of that?"

"Ay! Can you?" demanded Dalkeith fiercely, at the Colonel's other elbow.

"To be sure, he can't," O'Grady asserted from across the table. "Nobody can. The lawfulness of assassination is not to be questioned when it's after promoting the interest of Church or State. Didn't the Holy Father, himself, head a thanksgiving procession, and weren't the guns of Sant' Angelo fired in honour of the massacre of St Bartholomew?"

"That is not an argument that will win you sympathy in England for this deed."

"Sure it's the deed itself will win us all the sympathy we'll be needing."

Colonel Walton leaned back in his chair, with half-closed eyes, his face now impassive again. He was aware that he had aroused hostility, mistrust, even dread. He saw these emotions reflected on every face about him. He was aware of the steady hardness of the eyes with which Glenleven from the table's foot was watching him.

Upon that heat of repressed anger his voice fell cold and quietly.

"It is not worth while to pursue an argument that has become concerned with terms. Do not let us be deceived by quibbles. Call this thing by what name you will, the fact remains that we have here an assassination plot; just such a plot as that which failed two years ago, and for which some poor devils were hanged."

"Damme!" Sir Hamish fiercely interrupted him. It is not at all the same."

"In aim and in essentials it is, and because it is what it is, I tell you that it is foredoomed. Oh, have patience, sirs. Plots to assassinate kings have been as numerous almost as there have been kings in history. Yet very few kings have ever been assassinated. That is because, sooner or later, wittingly or unwittingly, there has been someone to betray the plot; and this again because sooner or later some one person's conscience has been aroused to revolt against the projected deed. Prendergass, who betrayed the last plot, was as stout a Jacobite as any of you. He loved King James and hated the Prince of Orange as deeply as any of you..."

He was interrupted by a sudden, sharp challenge from Glenleven.

"Are you not in this?"

"Oh, well – as any of us, then. Yet Prendergass was so appalled by the thought of murder that so as to avert it he betrayed his friends to his enemies."

"At least we've no Prendergass here," protested O'Grady, and added: "Glory be!"

"Unless you be one, Colonel Walton," came sternly from Glenleven. As the person who had introduced the Colonel, he would naturally be labouring under a sense of his responsibility.

The expression brought from the others an almost instant challenge to Colonel Walton to declare himself. Only Lady Lochmore held aloof, watching him ever with her dark eyes, which now were faintly wistful.

The Colonel's glance never faltered. He tossed back the lace from his fine hand, and again raised it in an appeal for patience.

"I am a professional soldier," he began. "Professional soldiers by concerning themselves ever with the practical and excluding the emotional, are vouchsafed a vision unclouded by such enthusiasms as very naturally are yours. If I am to serve you at all, I beg that you will hear me patiently. You know that I have spent some months on my travels through this England. Had I made the same tour two years ago, I should have found weapons collected, men assembled and sometimes even secretly drilling; everywhere an air of preparation, of expectancy, of readiness for a general rising the moment the signal should be given. Then came the discovery of the Assassination Plot; and of how effectively that blow quelled the Jacobite ardour it has been mine in these months to realize. Here in London, it is not to be denied that a certain Jacobite spirit is astir, although I do not believe that it touches the masses. But even if it did, it would be folly to be deceived by it. London is not England. Let me tell you what I found everywhere in the shires. The weapons are buried or hidden, the men disbanded, the expectancy dead. Anything done now would take the country by surprise, find it unprepared. Presently, let us hope, that which is in all loyal hearts will begin to stir again: the desire to restore the rightful king. But any premature action such as you contemplate may scatter a fresh panic, and quench, perhaps for all time, the spirit that may be only just beginning to revive."

"Say, rather," cried Dalkeith, "that it will prove a spark to fire the train and explode the mine."

"But if it fail?"

"It cannot fail," Sir Hamish answered him impetuously. "In the last plot there were too many. In this there are only a chosen few. Last time it was the extent of the preparations that defeated the aim. This time we prepare nothing but the cardinal deed, and leave the rest to happen in the way of nature, inevitably as it must."

"And when the rotten orange has been squeezed," added O'Grady, "events will follow of themselves to bring the King to his own again."

Her ladyship leaned towards the Colonel. "Are you convinced? Are we to count upon you?"

He looked at her, and smiled with his lips. His steady eyes remained grave.

"You may count upon me, convinced or not."

But Glenleven was not satisfied. "There is no counting upon any man who is without conviction."

O'Grady cut in as if to mitigate the hostility of his lordship's tone. "Faith, now, Colonel, Glenleven's right in that, so he is. Glory be, what more conviction will you be needing? This time the sword'll fall truly and without any kind of warning."

"Even as their sword fell at Glencoe, yet not as treacherously," said her ladyship, and her mouth grew hard.

Colonel Walton was under no necessity to ask for an explanation. Too well he knew from Invernaion the significance of that allusion.

If he had startled them by his frankly avowed hostility to the business that linked them, he had reassured them at least in part by showing that the real basis of his hostility was the persuasion that it could not forward the interests of King James. It remained to render that reassurance complete, and to this he addressed himself.

He began by asserting clearly that since the business upon which they were engaged, rightly or wrongly, was the business of King

James, he would not refrain from joining hands with them if they could show him in what his association was necessary to the prosperity of their cause.

It was Claybourne, who in his quiet, gentle way seemed in some sort the dominant spirit there, who answered him.

Once the blow fell, and the expected rising logically followed, a man of strong character and wide military experience would be necessary to combine, co-ordinate and generally order the forces that would lie at their disposal. Such a man they accounted Colonel Walton; and it was chiefly because of this that they had invited him to join them. Claybourne went on to speak of the recompense that would await the Colonel from the restored King, the high office in the State to which he might reasonably aspire, and to which he would not aspire in vain; such an office as that which Marlborough had forfeited by his treachery.

Being launched upon this side of the question, his lordship had that to say to the others which was of a similar nature. Perhaps it was to counteract any doubt which the Colonel's criticisms might have sown, that he now reminded each of those men of the great reward awaiting him when the King should come to his own again. Thus was it gradually revealed to Colonel Walton how self-interest was with them the spur to a loyalty whose roots were firmly set in personal ambition.

Veiling his contempt, he permitted them to assume that he shared their enthusiasm, so as to allay the last doubt concerning his attitude and to restore some confidence in him even to the perturbed Glenleven.

The initiation of Colonel Walton having been thus satisfactorily completed, and this being the only business for which they had assembled on that occasion, they pledged the King Over the Water once more by way of a closing ritual, and on that departed.

Chapter 16

Vain Remonstrances

Those eight conspirators – in which number Colonel Walton is now included – held meetings almost daily thereafter at Lochmore House. This frequency they accounted necessary because daily now it was expected that announcement would be made of the definite date of King William's departure for Holland.

The meetings, however, were productive of nothing but talk, all of it very high-sounding, but none of it in any way constructive. For what was to follow after the assassination, no sort of provision appeared to be made. They seemed to rest in the faith that once King William were dead the country would rise of itself to demand the recall of the rightful, exiled monarch, and that it would be time enough then to marshal the forces that were to spring as if by magic into view.

Whilst Colonel Walton would have been prepared to admit that some such consummation was not entirely impossible, yet he would have expected such a group of men as this to be concerned with the preparation of detailed plans for dealing with the situation when and if it arose, and the assignment to each of a definite post with pre-determined duties.

That no attempt was made to do anything of the kind, that no thought of it even appeared to exist, increased the disdain in which he held them as conspirators.

Meanwhile their sterile meetings continued, and continued to be sterile, because from Court came no such precise word of King William's journey as they were eagerly awaiting.

When word did at length come, in the last days of May, it was of a character to throw the plotters into a flurry of consternation.

It was Geoffrey Howard who brought it, straight from Court. The little weasel-faced man came amongst them as pale as the lace at his throat. He trembled and stammered in his excitement.

"Bad news," he announced to them. "The worst, in fact. I've just learnt at Kensington that the Prince of Orange's departure for the Hague is postponed. Indefinitely postponed."

His first two words had led them to fear something worse than this. Perceiving now the relief on their countenances, and the supercilious smiles of one or two, the peppery little man became angry.

"Damme! Don't you realize what it means?"

"It means what you say," said Claybourne. "Postponement."

"Ha! And you think that's a matter to be taken coolly? What, pray, does postponement mean at a time when he is so urgently required by the Dutch States? Is it a trifling matter, or has it some significance?"

This made them reflect. With reflection their faces lengthened, and presently they were looking at one another with uneasy eyes.

O'Grady chose to question the accuracy of Howard's information, and thereby put Howard in another passion. Did they suppose that he would bring them news of such gravity without first assuring himself beyond doubt that it was correct? He had obtained the information at the Palace directly from Cutts.

At this their uneasiness increased. Speculations began to be voiced about the table at which they sat in that panelled dining-room.

Was it possible that in spite of all their precautions, their project was discovered? That King William was informed not only of the existence of the plot, but of the occasion chosen for its execution?

Why else should he postpone a journey of such vital importance to him?

These were amongst the speculative questions they asked one another in varying terms.

Colonel Walton took no part in this jejune discussion. He sat back, with eyelids drooping sleepily over very watchful eyes. He dissembled in an air of gloomy thoughtfulness an alertness that missed not only no word, but no inflexion.

Of all those present the ever-reckless, volatile O'Grady was the only one, he observed, who refused to be intimidated.

"Och, now, are we to start at shadows?" he demanded, to steady the increasing disquiet. "There may be a dozen reasons of which we know nothing for the postponement. So there may. And as for discovery, faith, unless there's a traitor here amongst us, how could that be possible at all?"

"But is a traitor impossible?" wondered Glenleven darkly. "After all, there was Prendergass in the last plot, and... "

Stuart of Meorach interrupted him impatiently. "What are ye saying, man?"

"What, indeed?" murmured the gentle Claybourne, his countenance shocked.

"It's just blathering he is," said O'Grady, a sneer on his nut-cracker face. "Child's talk! Would ye be after looking for a traitor here? There's never a man among us whose loyalty hasn't been put to the test, Glenleven. And it's not myself is the only one to bear the scars of wounds taken in the service of King James."

Glenleven inclined his head, partly convinced. "My suspicions were perhaps too ready," he admitted. "But it is possible that there may have been an imprudence."

Lady Lochmore looked round with eyes of intercession.

"If any here is conscious of it, let him frankly admit it now, so that we may take our measures."

None answered her until Colonel Walton broke the silence he had hitherto preserved. He addressed them generally. "Measures should be taken in any event. At least such measures as will remove her ladyship from danger." Then he turned to her. "Would it not be prudent if you were to leave town for the present? Withdraw into the country, and dissociate yourself from us?"

O'Grady's hard stare seemed to be questioning him. But although conscious of it, he continued: "If there are risks to be run... "

And then her ladyship, herself, interrupted him. "I'll run them, if you please, Colonel. My presence here is necessary."

"Necessary?" His question was an expostulation. "To receive messages from your brother? Surely that is a function any one of us may discharge equally well. If your cousin Glenleven were to remain, and... "

"It is not enough, as Glenleven knows." She was firm. "My place is here, Colonel, and nothing will move me from it. Certainly not an alarm for which there may be no real grounds."

"That's what I say," O'Grady supported her. "There can be no real grounds for all this panic. No grounds at all."

To the Irishman, Colonel Walton paid little heed. His whole attention was given to her ladyship. And so determined and final was her tone that he realized the idleness of saying more at the moment, and in the presence of those others. He contrived, however, that day to linger on, after the company had departed, and her ladyship seemed nowise reluctant that he should do so. If she did not invite, at least she did not discourage it.

Alone with him in that panelled chamber, where the chairs stood awry about the table from which the conspirators had risen, he renewed and elaborated his arguments for her withdrawal from town until they should be assured that no real danger existed.

She went to occupy a window-seat whence she could overlook the garden and the river and the green fields of the Southwark shore beyond, all bright in the late May sunshine. She looked up at him standing tall, elegant and earnest beside her. A faintly quizzical smile played over her ivory-tinted face.

"I thought that I had already answered all this. I am touched, sir, by your concern. But it is perhaps less flattering than you suppose it."

"Flattery, madam, is a coarse incense to be burnt by cheap gallants on the altar of vulgar divinities."

"Lord, sir! You are didactic," she mocked him.

"It is my desire to be plain."

"You scarcely succeed in it."

"That is to come. My aim, madam, is not to flatter; but to save."

"To save? To save, do you say? That is vastly kind. But I am in no need of saving."

"Madam, you are in urgent need of it. You may be in gravest peril. Do not be deceived by the assumption that there may be no real grounds for alarm. This postponement of the departure of the Prince of Orange is a sure sign that the government has come by knowledge of the plot against him."

She looked at him gravely. "You are very positive. Why? Surely it is just your fears that direct your conclusions. How can you possibly be so certain that there are no other reasons? But I will not attempt to persuade you. If you see nothing but danger and discovery ahead, you are not obliged to linger. The way is open for you to depart."

He shrugged. "I am committed," he said, which was pure truth. "Besides, it is not my possible fate we are considering; but yours. This is no woman's work."

She looked up again, in irritation now, a flush creeping into her cheeks. But at sight of the gravity and kindliness in his grey eyes, the emotion partly melted.

"I am a Macdonald," she said quietly.

"Does that make you less than a woman?"

"It makes me something more than many a man."

He stared at her white fierceness. "Compassionate my dullness; my ignorance. I am not a Scot and have never been in Scotland. To be a Macdonald...? What is it, then?"

She rose to answer him, and her voice vibrated. "It is to be of the blood of those who were foully, cruelly, treacherously massacred at Glencoe by order of this Dutch usurper."

Breathlessly, in a few words, she told a tale that he already knew; the tale of that foul deed, whose real authors were Stair and

131

Breadalbane and Argyll, performed in the name of a King, who – as the Colonel believed – probably knew the truth of it as little as any man in England.

"You speak of what we plan as murder. How, I wonder, would you speak of that? For that was murder, indeed; ruthless, wholesale butchery, foul and treacherous."

Her eyes seemed to blaze upon him from her white face.

Suddenly on a gust of emotion she swept past him to a buffet on which stood a bowl of oranges. She snatched one up, and held it out in her enveloping hand. "To this, sir, am I pledged. This do I desire to see accomplished. In this must I lend my aid." And so violently did she clench her hand upon the fruit that it burst within her grasp and the juice of it squirted in all directions. With a gesture of disdain and disgust, she flung the yellow pulp into the empty fireplace, and sought a napkin for her hand.

Colonel Walton was touched, despite himself, by a display of emotion as sincere and powerful as its expression was histrionic. He bowed his head a little.

"Madam, you help me to understand yourself."

"You thought I plotted for the love of plotting, or so that I might derive importance from it, or profit by it afterwards."

"Like your associates? No, no. I knew there was this nobler spur for you."

"A spur, indeed. A goad. Glencoe! That was the foulness that proved the man; the foulness that calls for vengeance to every surviving Macdonald in the world."

The Colonel fetched a sigh. The moment was not one in which to present his beliefs that King William was no conscious author of that crime.

"Your anger may be righteous, and righteous the desire to see so great a wrong avenged. Righteous, too, your zeal to see the lawful king restored. But it still remains that you are a woman, and that it is not for a woman to have active part in these things."

"There were women at Glencoe."

"And King William's butchers did not discriminate. Be that your warning. They will not discriminate here if we are discovered. You know the fate of regicides, in fact or in intent? It is common to quarter them, and to exhibit the quarters in conspicuous places. A head on Temple Bar, a leg or so at Aldgate…"

"Oh, this is brave of you! This is gallant!" Her sudden scorn was fierce and withering. "You would make a coward of me by such images…"

"None could do that," he broke in. "I but ask you to leave men's work to men. The risk for you is now too grave. The consequence of discovery too horrible. Nor are you really necessary for the success of this enterprise, as those others know." He grew suddenly hot and vehement, a rare thing with him, whose cold self-command had passed, in France, into a byword. "I implore you not to suffer yourself further to be used."

There was a moment's silence in which she continued in the stricken astonishment his words had brought her. "Used?" she said slowly, frowning, "I am being used?"

"By those who permitted you to enter into this, so that your house might serve them for a rallying ground, so that your brother might be a tool for the accomplishment of their own ambitions. For that is the truth, the only truth I have gleaned from all their talk at these meetings. It is all wrong. Most wrong of Glenleven, who is your kinsman, allied to you by blood; and of Claybourne, who offers to me the command of an army, to Dalkeith a secretaryship of State, and something else to each of these self-seekers all of whom, like himself, serve the King that they may serve themselves. That they should imperil themselves for the chance of profit I can condone. But not that they should recklessly imperil you in their desperate gamble."

She stared at him wide-eyed.

"Are you mad?" she asked him.

He recovered his calm, and answered her: "It happens, madam, that I reverence you; and I would have you reverenced by others; and not used by any; still less imperilled by any."

"I thank you, sir." She was ironical. "I am flesh and blood. I do not live in an altar-niche. And I am in no need of champions."

"Neither is the Virgin Mary. But there are those who champion her none the less."

She moved past him, straight and lissom, to the window again, with a quickened heave of the breast to betray the perturbation he had stirred.

"When do you reach your conclusion, sir? For I must suppose there is a conclusion to all this." There was a hardness in her voice.

He addressed himself to the graceful back she had turned upon him. "I conclude, madam, where I began; by imploring you to depart at once into the country; or, better still, cross to France, and leave us men to confront the peril that already may be nearer than you suspect."

"You do not hesitate to ask me to forsake these friends who trust me?"

The strength of his feelings betrayed him into heat again.

"Say rather these men who play upon the sense of wrong under which you labour, so as to make you a party to their schemes; who use you; you, and Invernaion who is to strike the blow that will open for them the door of opportunity; these men who would have you continue to stake your own and your brother's life upon their gamble, for their profit, even when discovery already shows how the dice must fall against you."

"You speak of discovery as a fact, when it is still no more than a possibility."

"Even as a possibility only, their manhood should take shame to imperil you, as they shall hear from me perhaps when this adventure is ended. For, however it ends, if they and I escape the consequences, I shall have that to tell them which may help them to a better understanding of themselves."

She wheeled sharply to face him. "You do not want for faith in yourself."

"I do not, madam. Will you think over what I have said?"

"Not an instant. I forgive you the impertinence because of the mistaken concern in which I perceive it to have been practised."

He took a step towards her, then her gesture checked him. "No more on this subject, Colonel Walton. I am tired. I beg that you will leave me."

He hesitated yet a moment, then fetched an audible sigh, brought his heels together, and bowed.

"Your ladyship's obliged servant," he said, and obediently departed.

Chapter 17

The Wrath of Glenleven

Late that same night Glenleven came to Lochmore House. Her ladyship had already retired. Nevertheless, upon hearing of his presence, she rose again, and wrapped in a bed-gown, her lustrous black hair confined in a lace coif, she descended to the library, where he waited.

"You are very opportune, Jamie, in spite of the hour. I had thought tonight of sending for you."

His eyes, very grave and searching, pondered the signs of trouble which were obvious in her countenance.

"I was, myself, uneasy on your account," he said. "So uneasy that I could not sleep until I had seen you." He made a pause before adding: "Colonel Walton remained here with you today after all had left."

She raised her brows. "You are well informed."

"I have seen Claybourne since," he explained. "Saving Colonel Walton, he was the last to go. He told me that he had left the Colonel with you."

Something quizzical in her glance drew a faint flush to that narrow face of his.

"Do not suppose me jealous," he cried out. "All that is over. You have seen, I hope, that I am not one of those tiresome men who cannot take 'no' for an answer."

"I am not supposing it."

Indeed, she had little cause to do so. Glenleven's pursuit of her, so ardent while it lasted, had ceased completely over a year ago. The rebuff he had received when he hastened to her so confidently after his release from the Tower had been the last that he had courted. On the heels of that, his fear of being dealt with by act of attainder had come to preoccupy him. But even when his fear had been laid to rest, after that visit of his to Kensington and his long interview with Portland, of which he could never bear to speak, he had not again attempted to resume the wooing of Ailsa Lochmore.

It was evident to her, and she was relieved by it, that he had at last accepted her refusal as definite and final.

For months thereafter he had been at no pains to seek her, and she had seen him merely at rare intervals, when he had been strictly cousinly. It was only of late that they had been brought once more into close relations by this plot of which Glenleven was really the chief architect.

Because of what the plot owed to his invention and energy, and because it opened the way to the accomplishment of what to her, as to her brother, seemed almost a sacred duty, she had shown Glenleven a greater warmth than ever before. Nor had he curtailed it by any attempt to take advantage of it and reach for more than was plainly offered. He had earned her increased esteem by his circumspection, and also because, as it seemed to her, he had thrown himself into these labours and these fresh perils out of a selfless devotion which looked for no reward. In a similar warm esteem had she held each of those whom he had associated with himself.

Colonel Walton's words to her that day, pondered at leisure after her cool dismissal of him, had come to disturb that good opinion. However loftily, almost disdainfully, she might have listened to the Colonel, what he had said was, nevertheless, a seed which had since thrust roots into her mind.

The more she considered, the more confirmation did she discern in the facts, themselves, for Colonel Walton's strictures upon the motives actuating her fellow-conspirators.

The genial, courtly Claybourne, who secretly held from King James a commission, which entitled him to regard himself as his exiled majesty's ambassador to the Jacobites in England, saw himself already as a kingmaker. When the King should come to his own again Claybourne confidently counted upon holding under him a position of such power and influence as that which Bentinck held under King William. And as with Claybourne, so with each of the others. Each was intent upon the rich morsel that should fall to him from the restoration banquet.

She recalled having heard them come to the verge of altercation over the great offices of State they considered should be distributed amongst them when the restoration should be accomplished.

Particularly, and naturally, did her thoughts dwell upon Glenleven, both as her kinsman and as the real author of the plot, the man who had suggested to Invernaion when and how the blow might be struck. She remembered the reduced state of Glenleven's fortunes; she recalled the venal arguments by which, after Glencoe, her brother had re-awakened loyalty in this kinsman who had taken, from venal motives, the oath of allegiance to the usurper. A doubt entered her mind whether he, whom she had regarded as so selfless in his devotion, were in reality as self-seeking as Colonel Walton asserted.

Nor was it on the score of venality alone that in her mind she began to reprobate him and those others. They would, after all, scarcely have been human had they been so far removed from worldliness as to look for no recompense from the King they were to restore. But Colonel Walton had charged them with something more. He had accused them of using her and Invernaion for their own ambitious ends. Had he accused them of using her alone, she would have let the accusation pass, even though she might perceive the truth of it. But that they should use Invernaion, that they should employ him as their tool, that they should imperil his life, so that they might climb, making perhaps of his dead body a stepping-stone to the eminences they coveted; this was an intolerable, torturing thought to that loving sister.

It was the profound trouble into which this thought had cast her which prompted the notion of sending for Glenleven, and made her welcome now his coming.

At the same time, the anxiety that obviously must be urging him when he sought her at this hour was mystifying. It was the more mystifying since he disavowed – and truthfully, in her view – all notion that jealousy was his spur.

"You had thought of sending for me," he was slowly saying, and asked her bluntly: "Why?"

She waved him to a chair, and herself sank to another, drawing the rich, fur-trimmed robe about her. But instead of answering, she counter-questioned him.

"You were uneasy on my account. So uneasy that you could not sleep. Why?"

He stared at her. "My God! Are we to fence with each other?"

Her dark brows met in a frown. Her glance was very straight and level.

"That's an odd question, Jamie. Does your conscience make you perceive a reason why we should? You seek me at an unconscionable hour. I am entitled to an explanation, and I am waiting for it so that I may return to bed."

For a moment he seemed nonplussed. Then leaning forward, his elbow on his knee, he spoke quickly.

"Since you are in haste, then, I must be blunt, out of concern for you. What had Colonel Walton to say to you when he hung behind today?"

She continued to look at him straightly for a moment or two.

"What do you fear, Jamie?" she asked at last.

He straightened himself abruptly. It was a movement of exasperation. "Will you answer no question of mine?" he broke out.

"Oh, yes. When you ask me one in which I can perceive your concern."

"I see," he said. He was oddly sharp and irritable. "If you tell me that Colonel Walton stayed behind to make love to you, then it is not

139

my concern; and that is the end of the matter. I may go sleep in peace."

Her eyes flashed angrily. Her lips parted to speak. Then, as if the thought to be uttered were checked and changed, they curled a little. In a voice of obvious restraint she answered him. "That was not Colonel Walton's purpose. He stayed to represent to me again my danger."

"Danger!" He snorted, contemptuously angry. "What danger?"

"The danger of being hanged, drawn and quartered, of course. The quarters conspicuously exhibited. A head on Temple Bar, a leg or so on Aldgate."

"What?"

"Why do you cry out? You'll not deny that this danger exists?"

"If it exists at all, it exists for every one of us."

"But more particularly for Ian who is your catspaw."

"Was that Colonel Walton's suggestion?" Glenleven was suddenly livid.

"I do not think he used that word. But it contains the truth. Does it not? For every one of you there will be great profit if restoration follows upon the death of William of Orange. Claybourne looks to play the part of Monk, and already apportions among you the high offices you are to fill. I do not know what is to be your office, Jamie; but I do know the dilapidated state of your fortunes and how richly a King's gratitude will repair them. It is Ian, however, who is to strike the blow devised by you; and Ian may well leave his own life in the business so as to make the fortunes of you others who sit snugly here at home. That is the real end to which Ian's righteous desire to avenge Macdonald blood is being used."

Glenleven got up, shaking with passion. "As God's my life, this knave has schooled you famously."

"No, no," she said. "He merely pointed the way. The rest I have since perceived for myself."

"And you intend?" He was peremptory.

She made a little gesture of helplessness. "I have no intentions…
yet. I have told you that it was in my mind to send for you. But now
I ask myself why."

He stood looking down at her in silence, and gradually now his
manner changed. The fury faded out of him, until he had become
once more his coldly courteous self. Not until then did he permit
himself to speak.

"I think that I can supply the answer," he said with comparative
quiet. "You desired to test on me these doubts that have been sown
in you."

"It may have been that," she admitted. "I scarcely know."

"Of course it was that. What else could it be? I think I understand.
This fellow Walton has the presumption to be in love with you."

She would have interrupted him, but he held up a hand to check
her. "I have read it in his eyes each time they look on you." His smile
was quietly scornful. "That emotion makes him fearful where you are
concerned. And fear magnifies and distorts all things.

"Listen," he said, and in that musical, persuasive voice, from
which he excluded now all harshness of passion, he set himself to
combat these new-born prejudices, to expose the error and injustice
that lurked in them.

For those who actively laboured for the restoration of King James
there might well be rewards. That was what usually happened in
such cases. Neither more nor less. Was it, then, to be pretended that
because of those rewards men were not to labour to restore a rightful
king? If they were venal, then every man who had ever set his hand
to the righting of a wrong such as existed now in England was also
venal. She saw, he hoped, the puerility of such a contention.

To accuse them of making a tool of Invernaion for the gratification
of their own ambitions, and to imply that they did not share the risks
Invernaion ran in this undertaking was fantastically unjust. Did she
forget how he, himself, had gone to the Tower, and very nearly to the
headsman, for conspiring in a degree no deeper than the present?
And if the plot should fail, as plots were always liable to fail,
especially when doubts such as Walton had sown came to weaken

resolve, did she suppose that he would again escape? Whatever the fate of the others, his doom would not lie in doubt.

That argument shook her a little.

But Glenleven had not yet done. He could trace these slanders uttered by Walton to their very source. The Colonel's military experience and acknowledged talents made him valuable to them. Walton, however, was a soldier by trade, a self-confessed mercenary who made no secret of the fact that his loyalty was to the hand that paid him. Had she forgotten how this had been discussed when it was first proposed to bring Walton into their enterprise? Glenleven had enlisted him by holding out to him the prospect of the great reward that would await his labours.

Because Walton had been persuaded by venal arguments, he defamed them all by the assumption that they were all in like case, that venality was their only incentive. And now at the first negligible shadow of danger, because of his feelings for her ladyship, Colonel Walton used that assumption as an argument to detach her from the undertaking.

This specious reasoning lightened her doubts still further.

To set a crown to his persuasive advocacy, Glenleven made an appeal to her emotions. He spoke of Glencoe and of the sacred duty it placed upon every living Macdonald. In the fulfilment of that duty, he, for one, would flinch before no risk. He spoke of Invernaion as an avenging angel, an incarnation of overdue Macdonald vengeance upon the chief dastardly author of that massacre of Macdonalds. The real danger to Invernaion lay in any faltering here, in their failure to support him with timely and accurate information. The very opportunity now chosen was one that reduced the risk to an almost negligible point. And Invernaion, he reminded her, was not alone over there. He was well supported, his measures would be well and cautiously taken, and he would be given every assistance.

He was still talking in this strain when she made an end of argument.

"It is enough, Jamie. I have been, perhaps, too ready to listen to the voice of fear."

"You mean the voice of Walton."

"If you will. It may well be that regard for me has made him magnify the dangers. You have supplied me with answers for him if he should renew his arguments."

"Of that," said Glenleven, "he shall have no opportunity."

She looked up quickly, moved by the sinister note in his voice.

"What do you mean?"

"Just that. I owe a duty to you in the absence of your brother. This man's presumption must be punished."

"You've changed your views since you arrived," she said, and grew severe. "I am in no need of champions, Jamie. I can punish presumption for myself."

He bowed coldly. "So be it. But I still owe a duty to myself. This man has defamed me."

"That is an overstatement. It is something for which no word of mine gives you authority."

"This is frivolous." His patience was slipping from him again. "And anyway, I do not intend that he shall recommence; that he shall again attempt to… "

She was on her feet, alarm plain in her face. "What do you intend to do?"

"What does a gentleman do to a slanderer?"

She advanced upon him. She gripped his arm with a strength he had never suspected in her slim white hand.

"Jamie, you shall not! I forbid it. You must not make a quarrel of it. This matter is to go no further."

He held himself very straight as he gave her back glance for glance. His eyes were hard to the point of cruelty, and there was a cruel set to his mouth. "Your concern for this adventurer supplies an added reason why I should kill him."

"Kill him!" she echoed. "Kill him!"

"Oh, but in proper form." A wicked little smile broke on his white face. "For murder I stoop to nothing less than a king. A friend of mine shall wait upon Colonel Walton in the morning."

"You must not, I say. You must not." Vehemently she shook the arm she held. "I will not have it."

"It distresses me to go against your wishes, sweet cousin. But I must be the guardian of my honour." Abruptly, roughly, he wrenched his arm from her grasp. "Good night!" he savagely flung at her, and strode past her to the door.

She swung round where she stood, distressed, in panic.

"Jamie! It is possible that he may kill you. Have you thought of that?"

On the threshold the libertine, who by his swordsmanship had kept himself unpunished, turned. He smiled at that poor attempt to frighten and so deter him.

"Your concern is very sweet," he said, in bitter sarcasm. "All things are possible, of course. But that, at least, is a thing that is not probable."

He passed out, and closed the door before she could find an answer.

A moment she remained where he had left her, undecided, wringing her hands. Then she ran to the door, pulled it open, and called after him.

"Good night," his voice answered her from the gloom of the hall, and the slamming of the house-door set a full stop to that period.

Chapter 18

The Encounter

Major O'Grady sought Colonel Walton in his Covent Garden lodging, and found him at breakfast in bed-gown of flowered silk over frilled shirt and satin breeches, his cropped head swathed in a kerchief of blue silk, with Lavernis in attendance.

"Ye're early astir, Major."

The Irishman's dark face looked more sinister than ever. "Needs must when the devil drives. What's your quarrel, now, with Glenleven?"

The Colonel showed surprise at the question. "I am aware of none."

"Faith, then, ye soon will be. For, bedad, he's on his way to you now to settle it. And since he don't choose that the town should be after knowing the details, he proposed to me that I should be with you against your need of a friend. Hence the intrusion at such an hour."

The Colonel stared for a moment. "I am honoured by your support, sir," he said with cold formality. He liked O'Grady rather less than any of his fellow-conspirators, which is to say that he disliked him considerably.

"A glass of hock, Major?"

"And why not, faith?" The Major brimmed himself a bumper.

The Colonel waved Lavernis from the room, and went on with his breakfast.

O'Grady sat down. "It's ill done of Glenleven, so it is. And I'm hoping you'll reason him out of his humour."

"If the gentleman is within easy reach of reason."

"I've never known a swordsman to be that. Usually he accounts it cowardly; being sure to kill his man."

"And Glenleven comes in that conviction, does he?"

"That's his assertion. Bad cess to it!"

The Colonel sighed. "I hope you esteem me well enough, Major, to send a handsome wreath to my funeral."

The Irishman scowled at him. "It's wrong ye are to treat the matter lightly. I wouldn't in your place."

"But, then, ye're not in my place. Be thankful."

Lord Glenleven came in briskly, ushered by Lavernis and followed closely by Stuart of Meorach.

The Colonel flung down his napkin, and rose to receive them.

His lordship was direct, abrupt and frosty.

"Colonel Walton, it has come to my knowledge that you have said that which hurts my honour. Need I be more particular?"

The Colonel was urbane. "Why no. Nor yet so anxious to meet trouble."

"It's a characteristic of my race."

"But are you sure that it is prudent?"

"More so than backbiting, Colonel Walton."

"Backbiting, my lord? Do you impute that to me?"

"You don't like the imputation?"

"I find it harsh. But no matter. And I forget my manners. A glass of wine, Glenleven?"

"Curse your wine."

The Colonel looked at him, sadly pensive. "Ye're determined not to be civil?"

Glenleven exploded. "Damme! D'ye suppose I'm here to be civil?"

"It would be prudent."

"Prudent? Oh, aye!" He sneered. "Ye're in love with prudence on a sudden. Had you practised it in your criticisms of me yesterday there'd be less need for it now."

"There is always need for it, my lord, believe me."

"Ay, for cowards," said his lordship, and waited to see the colour rise in the Colonel's pale face. But he waited in vain. The Colonel remained unruffled, looking down from his fine height upon the shorter man.

"Not only for cowards, I assure you. Shall we be sensible, Glenleven? Whatever your quarrel with me, is it not your duty and mine to declare an armistice until the matter demanding our alliance is concluded?"

"Faith, now, that's a sensible suggestion," put in O'Grady.

But Glenleven, clearly, was not of the same opinion. "To be frank, I am none so comfortable in this alliance; and we might not, ourselves, survive it. That, I believe, was the opinion you expressed. You spoke of quarterings, too. Most delicate."

"If we do not survive, will this our difference matter?"

Glenleven showed exasperation. "You're cursedly reluctant. Will this quicken you?" And he swept his feathered hat across the Colonel's face.

The Colonel fell back a pace to save his eyes. He remained straight and stiff, but showed no sign of intimidation. Glenleven did not know that it was said in France of Colonel Walton that he had never refused a challenge, and never killed an adversary. He sighed. "You're too hot, Glenleven, for a good plotter. But have with you. Give me leave to get my coat."

Imperturbable he bowed and went out, calling Lavernis to attend him. When he returned, in coat and periwig and wearing a sword, he found an altercation in progress and O'Grady clamorous.

"I tell you it's ill done, Glenleven, so it is. Sure if one of ye's killed, the other is arrested and the devil knows where the inquiries will end or what may be ferreted out."

"Spare yourself, O'Grady," said the Colonel. "No one will be killed this morning."

Glenleven turned sharply to look down his nose at him, Stuart of Meorach, drawing a rash conclusion, expressed it in contempt: "Are ye not coming, then?"

The Colonel bowed, and waved them on. "I follow, if you will lead, sirs."

They paused to stare at him. Then Glenleven and Sir Hamish went out. The Colonel followed with O'Grady.

They came out of the shadow of the Piazza into the sunshine, and made their way by a pleasant lane to the fields behind Lincoln's Inn.

"The Devil fly away with me if I understand you," the Major grumbled, as he walked with the Colonel a few paces behind the others.

"In what am I mysterious?"

"This concern, now, for Ailsa Lochmore. Pure sentimentality, so it is; and there's no room for that when you're engaged in such business as ours."

Colonel Walton disdained to argue. The Major grumbled on. "It's mighty ill ye're behaving. Both you and Glenleven."

"It distresses me not to merit your approval, Major."

"Oh, curse your sneers."

They came by a gate into a field where sheep had grazed the turf to a serviceable surface. They found a smooth space behind a screen of shrubs, and made ready swiftly and almost without words.

The Colonel removed his baldrick, stripped off his coat, and bound up the long black curls of his periwig. Then, sword in hand, he studied the ground and the light until Glenleven approached, and they got to work.

His lordship attacked vigorously, revealing a skill, speed and experience that more than compensated for the comparative shortness of his reach. It was plain also from the outset that he meant mischief. There was a grim, vicious purposefulness in his repeated lunges in carte following upon feintes in the low lines, and aiming straight at his opponent's heart.

But Glenleven, so easily victorious in so many encounters, neither knew nor yet realized with whom he had to deal. He construed into signs of timidity and conscious inferiority the fact that the Colonel fenced entirely on the defensive, and to this alone did he ascribe it that he found the opposing guard so firm and close. He was not disillusioned until he had attempted that high lunge of his once too often. The Colonel, expecting it, side-stepped to avoid the point, and so brought himself effortlessly within his adversary's guard. There, without apparent haste, he transfixed Glenleven's sword-arm.

The blade fell from his lordship's suddenly powerless hand. Sir Hamish, goggle-eyed, was instantly at his side.

The Colonel stepped back, lowered his recovered point, and, with head slightly inclined, stood watching his disabled opponent, his breathing as easy as when the combat started.

"I promised you that no one should be killed this morning. I keep my promises. All of them. I think it was perhaps a doubt of that which made you put this quarrel upon me. Perhaps you will perceive proof of it in my moderation." His manner was entirely deferential.

Glenleven, wincing with pain, looked into the Colonel's steady eyes.

And then, in the view of the onlookers, an odd thing happened. The expression of baffled fury gradually passed from his lordship's face. In the end he was smiling weakly.

"You are generous, damme! You might as easily have put your sword through my body."

"And sheltered myself afterwards by disclosing the grounds of our quarrel, or so much of them as would have ensured me the favour of Monsieur Bentinck. You perceive what a passport to his consideration that would have been; what profitable employment might then have awaited me. I hope your lordship perceives it."

The portent of Glenleven's conciliatory expression was momentarily lost in a stare of amazement instantly suppressed.

"Stab me!" he cried. "I do perceive it. I took you for a coward, Walton."

"Appearances are proverbially deceptive. Particularly mine."

He smiled.

Glenleven, a little bewildered, was scowling now, and gnawing his lip. Abruptly he put out his sound left hand. "I beg your pardon, Colonel Walton."

It was the Colonel's turn to frown and hesitate. But only for a moment. He took the proffered hand.

"You are generous in your turn," he said. "Oddly generous." And he went on quickly: "I regret the inconvenience caused you. But in a week all will be well again."

He assisted the clumsy Stuart to bandage the arm with a kerchief. Then he resumed his garments, took courteous leave, and departed with O'Grady.

The Irishman was still grumbling. "Faith, here's much ado about nothing. Glenleven might have begun where he ended, and saved himself a blood-letting."

"It's good for the humours," said the Colonel. "His lordship is a trifle hot for a Scotsman. And it'll be salutary for him to depend a little less in future upon his swordsmanship."

"Will somebody tell me why he wanted to quarrel with you at all?" quoth the intrigued O'Grady.

"You heard what he alleged. But I suspect that what you opined of me may be true of him: he is moved to sentimentality where Lady Lochmore is concerned."

"Arrah, now, that shaft's wide of the mark. It might ha' found it once. But that was long since. Anyway, over a year ago: before Glenleven's committal to the Tower. All the town knew then that he hoped to marry Ailsa Lochmore, and all the town was sure that in the end he would. But her ladyship disappointed both the town and Glenleven; for after his release from the Tower, which was thanks to what Ian Macdonald did, there was a sudden end of his pursuit of her. And that must have been by her ladyship's wish, for Glenleven would never have turned his back on the fortune she'ld ha' brought him. Not he, very near beggared as he is. Maybe she had scruples on the score of consanguinity; for they're over-kin to wed."

The Colonel nodded thoughtfully, and his chin remained sunk in his Steinkirk. The Irishman babbled on.

"Faith, it must have been like the torment of Tantalus to a man in his case, to see a fortune dangling before him and just out of reach. And faith it's not the only fortune that's near him and yet not near enough to grasp." O'Grady chuckled maliciously. "Isn't he heir to all the broad acres of Invernaion, and aren't they just as far from him?"

The Colonel checked in his stride to face the Irishman, his eyes solemn. "Heir to Invernaion! Of course he is. I had not realized it." For a moment, lost in thought, he continued to stare vacantly at the Major. Then he shrugged, and moved on, O'Grady stepping beside him. "Invernaion is no formidable obstacle to that inheritance, considering the mission in life he has made his own." He spoke almost sadly.

"Arrah, now! Aren't they linked together in it? If Invernaion falls, he certainly pulls Glenleven down, whoever else falls with him."

"None of which," said the Colonel, "explains why Glenleven having been in such anxiety to kill me, should afterwards be in a like anxiety to be friends again."

"To be sure, now, it's all just blathering nonsense, as I said from the first. Glenleven is just the devil himself on a point of honour. It's this being a swordsman makes him so. But honour being satisfied, there's a gentlemanly end to bad blood. Ye'll own his apology was a gracious one considering ye'd skewered his arm."

"So unnaturally gracious that I'm still seeking the reason for it."

"But haven't I just supplied it?"

"To your own satisfaction, Major. Not to mine." And he quoted: "*Timeo Danaos et dona ferentes.*"

"Now isn't it hard to please ye are, Colonel darling?" the Irishman grumbled, but himself fell silently thoughtful, and so remained until they parted in the neighbourhood of Covent Garden.

Coming alone into the Piazza, the Colonel found a hackney-coach drawn up before his lodging, and in his room, to his vast amazement, my Lady Lochmore, in cloak and wimple, awaiting him.

"Faith, it's a morning of surprises," was his rueful comment.

She had sprung up as he entered, her white face anxious. "Are you hurt?" she greeted him.

"Hurt, madam?" His dark brows went up in inquiry. But he lost some colour, and for once his breathing was quickened.

"Where is Jamie?"

"At the moment I could not answer with precision."

"You know what I am asking." She was fiercely impatient. She fluttered hither and thither in her agitation. "Your servant told me you went out together – four of you." She came up to him, and seized his arms. "What have you done with him?"

"Done with him?" The Colonel smiled. "We took a friendly walk in the fields. Glenleven had the misfortune to scratch his arm. Oh, but a trifling matter. What did you fear?"

Her dark eyes searched that quietly smiling countenance. Then becoming conscious of her tight grip of his arms, she loosed it, and stepped back.

"My God! How calm you are! Are you always so?"

"It is my endeavour. But I do not always succeed. Just now when I discovered you, I was alarmed. I am still. Under my calm I tremble for you. It is vastly indiscreet of Lady Lochmore to seek me here. Her good name… "

"Jamie had sworn that he would kill you."

"Men are so rash in the promises they will make a lady."

"You mock. But Jamie has a dangerous repute."

"Yet you were concerned for him?"

"For him!" she cried, and instantly checked. Conscious that her tone had betrayed the truth, the colour deepened in her face. She sought to retract, to cover her disclosure. "It was, sir, that I was distraught that my indiscretion should have been a source of quarrel between two men so precious to the cause."

"Your indiscretion? It was no more than that?" said he, although already in her bearing he held proof of what he asked.

"What else were you supposing?"

"It might have been a complaint of me to your kinsman."

She shook her head. "No. It was not that. Nor could Glenleven suppose it. I pondered your misgivings yesterday after you had gone. I saw the peril to the cause if they were well-founded. Jamie came to me, and in my heat I used some of the expressions you had used. He concluded that you had sown thoughts in me which never could have been my own. He knew that you had remained with me yesterday after the others had gone. He drew conclusions, and departed with the threat to kill you for defaming him. I think, too, he was uneasy about you in other ways; mistrustful of your loyalty. This morning my alarm had grown so that it gave me no peace. I came to warn you, and found I had hesitated too long and arrived too late."

He smiled upon the confusion of this high-spirited lady.

"I thank God it was just so," he said. "I would not for all the world have had it otherwise. I feared at first… But no matter what I feared. All that is over now. Glenleven and I are friends again."

She smiled at him in frank wonder. "You make all things possible."

"What I ask myself," he said, "is what part I had in this that could accomplish it. An odd fellow, your kinsman."

"In your hands, perhaps. You are one who succeeds with all and in all."

His eyes grew wistful. "Believe me, that is not my history at all. If it were, I should now… " He broke off and shrugged to imply that the thought was not worth uttering.

"You would what?"

He considered her, so slim and graceful, so proud of carriage, so black and white and so desirable. Her glowing eyes seemed clearly to invite him to confidences. For an instant he was in danger of succumbing to the temptation that assailed him. Then remembrance set a check upon him. Remembrance of several things.

She saw his face darken into gravity.

"Madam! I was forgetting. If your ladyship were found here!"

"Oh, what then? What then? Who cares?"

"Suffer me to care." He proffered his hand. "I will conduct you to your carriage."

Her eyes pondered him a moment, almost in sombre resentment, then, without another word, she took the proffered hand, and they went below in silence.

Bareheaded he stood at the door of her carriage to take his leave of her, "I am deeply touched, madam, by your solicitude," he said. "Deeply grateful for your explanation, and comforted by it."

"It was no more than due," she answered him, a sudden coolness in her voice.

The memory of that coolness abode with him when he had returned above and sat recalling her every spoken word. His long, handsome countenance was illumined by a wistful smile.

Chapter 19

The Avowal

By no means the least surprising feature of the affair between Colonel Walton and my Lord Glenleven was that it left upon the surface of things no trace of its passage. If their fellow plotters were aware of the quarrel and the meeting – and it is impossible to suppose on the part of O'Grady and Sir Hamish Stuart such discreetness as would leave them in ignorance – they made no allusion to it, and generally behaved as if nothing of the kind had occurred.

Glenleven, of course, bore upon his person the signs of the encounter. It was impossible for him to conceal a wound which compelled him to carry his arm in a sling. But the injury sustained by his pride, the pride of a man who had brought himself to be regarded as an invincible swordsman, he did tolerably succeed in dissembling. He may have winced a little under the scarcely suppressed, humorously scornful glance with which Lady Lochmore received him when next day he presented himself; but he let it pass in silence. Beyond a certain surliness there was no change perceptible in his demeanour when the plotters met some three days later at Lochmore House, in response to an urgent summons from her ladyship. Towards Colonel Walton, who was also present, his lordship observed a cool courtesy that scarcely differed from his normal chilly manner.

They assembled about a long table in the library, under the sombre painted eyes of the late Earl of Lochmore's puritanical sire.

The occasion of the summons proved to be the arrival from France of Mr Richard Hay, whom her ladyship presented to the company as the bearer of important tidings.

They beheld a young gentleman, tall and shapely, in an exaggeratedly curled red periwig, which went ill with his sallow complexion. He was very fine in green velvet, with shoulder-knots and gold-laced rosettes at his knees and on his high-heeled shoes, and he wore the ridiculous little moustache that was becoming fashionable with fops in France. He moved from the hips with the step of a dancing-master, and gesticulated and postured like a play-actor.

He was, Colonel Walton reflected with secret scorn, a figure to take the eye.

Mr Hay announced to them, with outrageous self-sufficiency of manner and tone, that he came from Saint Germains and Versailles, and that he was charged with messages to them from King James, King Louis, and Ian Macdonald of Invernaion. He made it clear that he regarded himself, and desired them to regard him, as a plenipotentiary, and there was more than a hint in his mincing, affected opening address to them that he expected them henceforth to submit to his direction the enterprise which they had in hand.

From King Louis he brought them a definite promise of troops once the country should have risen to restore its rightful King. To Colonel Walton at least there was nothing very novel in this. King Louis had been saying, quite sincerely, the same thing for a year and more.

From King James Mr Hay was the bearer of a lengthy message, which, when reduced to plain terms, amounted to little more than a blessing upon the labours they were putting forth on his behalf and a promise to reward those labours liberally once he should be back in his Palace at Whitehall.

Lastly the envoy came to the real business of his journey. He had brought a letter from Ian Macdonald, which whilst addressed to Lady

Lochmore was in fact intended for them all, since it contained information and instructions which concerned every person present.

This letter, Mr Hay announced, her ladyship would read to them; and with that announcement he at last sat down.

There was a stir of interest as her ladyship took up the sheet, and then an expectant silence. Upon that silence arose the quiet, level voice of Colonel Walton.

"Is it necessary or even desirable that your ladyship should read this letter to us?"

The frown with which she looked at him was one of inquiry. He was similarly considered by the others.

"Surely," said Claybourne, "we must hear it. How else are we to know its contents?"

"But is it necessary that we should?" the Colonel insisted. "Mr Hay speaks of information and instructions. I agree that we should all hear the instructions. But without knowing what the information is, I cannot judge the expediency of publishing it even here. I would suggest, with submission, that her ladyship should impart to us no more of the information than may be necessary for an understanding of the instructions."

The impatience about him was obvious and general. It was O'Grady who gave it expression.

"I don't know what may be in your mind, Colonel. But ye've heard Mr Hay. And what he said was that this letter is intended for us all, as of course it should be."

"I am not concerned with what Mr Hay has said. But with the fact itself."

"How, sir?" Mr Hay was purple. "Do you imply that I would say anything that is not in accord with the facts."

"Mr Hay, it is not my way to make implications. I am at pains to be plain. This letter is addressed to Lady Lochmore. That is the fact. In all the circumstances I must regard the letter itself as an indiscretion; a dangerous indiscretion. If it should have fallen into hostile hands… "

Her ladyship interrupted him.

"You are under a misconception, Colonel Walton. The letter is in cipher. It is a cipher devised by Ian, and employed between him and me."

Someone laughed at what he imagined to be the Colonel's discomfiture. But the Colonel was not discomfited.

"That merely lessens the imprudence. It does not extinguish it. I never yet saw a cipher that with a little trouble could not be deciphered. And the very employment of cipher can in itself be incriminating. But let that pass. Let us assume that the cipher covers the indiscretion of the actual letter. It is still for your ladyship to consider whether the information it contains is such as might be published here without peril to your brother."

"The devil fly away with me if I know what ye mean," said O'Grady, so hotly that it was plain he had no doubt at all of what was in the Colonel's mind.

Glenleven added in his most acid tone: "But that we have your assurance, Colonel Walton, that it is not your way to make implications, your meaning would be clear enough to me."

And then her ladyship intervened, and so averted the storm that seemed likely to break about the Colonel's head.

"Whatever may be in Colonel Walton's mind, sirs," she said, with quiet dignity, "I am satisfied that his intentions are of the worthiest. But the matter is one for my decision. Even Colonel Walton has admitted that. Now in my view the letter is not personal to myself, as you will, I think, agree when you have heard it. It is addressed personally to me merely for convenience and because the cipher employed renders this necessary. But it is clearly intended for you all. So that it but remains for me to read it."

Colonel Walton sank back in his chair with an air of resignation, indifferent to the mockingly triumphant sneers of one or two of his fellow-plotters. He had done his best to check what he feared might be the publication of a vital secret. To insist further would be merely to raise an unprofitable garboil.

Her ladyship in clear level tones began to read. As she proceeded the terms of the letter confirmed the Colonel's worst fears.

The instructions came first, and these were innocuous enough. Apparently they answered a question sent him by her ladyship on behalf of her associates. They amounted to little more than a strong recommendation to those who were in the plot, to employ the time of waiting in such measures among their Jacobite friends as would ensure that, once the blow were struck, leaders would be everywhere at hand, to encourage and promote a general rising. Invernaion entered into some details as to how they should proceed, so that preparation starting from themselves should spread in ever-widening circles throughout England.

Then Invernaion passed on to give that information about himself and his movements which Colonel Walton dreaded and would have suppressed. He announced that as the time for action must now be imminent, he was taking up his quarters at the Auberge du Soleil at Calais, under the assumed name of Richard Jerningham, and that he would wait there until he received from them the definite news of the sailing of the Prince of Orange for the Hague. Once he possessed this information, he would cross the frontier to join a group of loyal gentlemen who awaited him, to share with him the enterprise and to do what must be done in memory of Glencoe and so as to bring the rightful King to his own.

He closed with a strong recommendation to them not to lose a moment in informing him of the settled date of the sailing of William of Orange.

By the time her ladyship had come to the end of the letter, Colonel Walton's attitude towards the reading of it had been forgotten by his fellow-plotters in the excitement of seeing themselves at last confronted with the necessity of passing from words to deeds. Yet for the moment it was in words that they continued to deal.

Glenleven made an inflammatory speech, not one syllable of which was necessary or useful. Others followed more briefly, until all save only Colonel Walton had contributed something to this Jacobite symposium.

The Colonel was gloomily contemptuous of them, and in his heart appalled. The last and most important of the facts which Lord Portland desired to learn, the principal fact which Colonel Walton had been commissioned by him to ascertain, was now disclosed. Once armed with this knowledge the heavy hand of the law would no longer pause in its descent upon these plotters. This was not mere conjecture. Lord Portland, himself, had clearly stated, as Colonel Walton now remembered, that he waited only to make sure that the really troublesome and really dangerous Ian Macdonald of Invernaion could be laid by the heels before, in his own words, putting his foot on this wasp's nest of treason.

Sitting a little apart and very pensive, the Colonel became conscious some moments after O'Grady had ceased his brief final contribution to that unnecessary oratory that her ladyship's eyes were upon him, inviting him.

He looked round and found himself regarded by them all in expectant silence. He shook his head. "We have had too many words already." His ill-humoured tone was in itself a reproof. "Fewer would have been more prudent."

The self-sufficient, histrionic Mr Hay permitted himself to smile unpleasantly.

"In such a business as this, courage is of more account than prudence."

"They are not incompatible, sir," he was coldly answered. "With his own fortunes a man may be as reckless as lies within his humour. Not so with the fortunes of another, and particularly with the fortunes of a king, with which are bound up the fortunes of a people." He rose abruptly. "Since there's no more to say, I'll take the air, by your leave." And he went out alone by the open French window into the garden.

Their surprised, resentful glances followed him. Mr Hay, who accounted himself cavalierly used, was the first to speak. He was breathing hard, and there was a dark flush upon his countenance.

"But that man!" he cried, in the Gallic phraseology he affected. "Is he mad, then?" He heaved himself up impetuously, and moved to follow him. But Claybourne, rising, too, put himself in his way.

"Let be, sir! Let be!" He murmured, conciliatory.

"Let be? You can't have heard him. An explanation is necessary. Very necessary."

"Och, it's not necessary at all," drawled O'Grady. "Sure it's a man with notions of his own, and we may leave him to them. Anything else would scarcely, as he would say, be prudent. We'll not be wanting to attract attention."

The others by similar arguments prevailed upon Mr Hay; they wanted no disturbance such as that impetuous emissary seemed intent upon provoking. Thus Colonel Walton was left to pace the garden undisturbed. He was still pacing it, deep in thought, when, after they had all departed, her ladyship went to seek him there.

She was disposed to be distant with him.

"I have to reproach you with being less than civil. What was your reason? Was it even prudent in one who sets such store by prudence?" Thus uncompromisingly she challenged him.

"I could not trust myself to have patience with them. Is a king to be brought to his own again by vapourings? They're all of them greedy for office and rewards when the King comes back. But what will their indiscretions accomplish meanwhile? And then that mincing fellow Hay, tricked out like a Frenchman, to take the eye and advertise whence he comes at a time when every man from France is regarded with suspicion. That such a messenger was chosen is of a piece with the rest."

"And now you seem to be reproaching Ian. Surely you forget that men are not readily found to carry dangerous messages. Mr Hay is an old and valued friend of my brother's."

"Valued he may be: though, having seen and heard him, I can't imagine on what grounds. But as for old, I'll take leave to assert that when I left Saint Germains a year ago, this consequential fribble had not been heard of. And whatever the age or value of the friendship, where was the need to carry such a letter? So utterly unnecessary a letter?"

The Colonel's irritation bewildered her by its apparent lack of reason. It wore the aspect of petulance, the last fault she would have suspected in him.

"It is necessary that we should know my brother's whereabouts. How else are we to communicate with him?"

"The information could have come by word of mouth, like the royal messages."

She began to lose patience. "But don't you see that the letter served as an evidence of good faith to accredit the messenger."

Grudgingly he conceded the point; but he did not on that account depart from his main contention. "In that case, it should have been for yourself alone."

"The others have as good a title as I to guarantees."

And now it was he who manifested impatience, vehemently. "It is too grave a secret to be held by so many."

"They are all loyal hearts, sir."

"Too cursed loyal!" He was bitter, to her further astonishment. "Too notoriously loyal. All, saving perhaps Howard, are marked Jacobites, and they come here day after day, for no better purpose than to squeeze oranges, toast the King Over the Water, and rant like barnstormers. Not even the significant postponement of King William's sailing can restrain them. Do they suppose that this government is asleep or besotted? Do they really imagine that these constant comings and goings at Lochmore House have not brought you under observation? Has Bentinck no spies? Do you suppose that he is ignorant of the arrival in London of Mr Hay? Of whence he comes, and whom he visits?"

"Mr Hay has been allowed to pass freely."

"Which proves the opposite of what you all so complacently imagine. I tell you this, and no one has better cause to know it: every arrival at, and departure from, Saint Germains is known to Monsieur Bentinck almost as soon as it has taken place. Every man who leaves there for England is marked and watched. Let that help you to understand why the arrest of Mr Hay would have caused me less uneasiness than the liberty he enjoys."

"You do not apply this argument to your own case. You came from Saint Germains and do not seem to have been troubled by Monsieur Bentinck."

"You forget, ma'am, that it was well known at the time why I left France. I came home to take up a heritage, and so that I might be free to enjoy it I moved with a circumspection unknown to these hare-brains of yours. There is Claybourne proposing to send letters into Wiltshire, which may well be intercepted. There is Howard proposing to proselytize in the coffee-houses, as if all but Jacobites are deaf. There was Glenleven picking a quarrel with me whilst joined with me in such a task as this. If either of us had been killed, whither would inquiry have led?" He made a gesture of impatience. "I see no hope, no hope at all, for any undertaking conducted in such folly. And is there nothing more than folly to be feared? Loyal hearts, you say. Are you so sure that all are loyal? Are you so sure that amongst the seven of us there is not a betrayer?"

She recoiled in horrified amazement. "This is too much!" she protested. "What are you saying?"

"I remind you of a possibility never absent from such enterprises. Remember Prendergass."

"We have no Prendergass here."

"Can you be sure? Observe how history may be repeating itself. Because of Prendergass – at heart a very staunch and loyal adherent of King James – King William postponed his hunting. Is it so remotely improbable that it is because of another Prendergass, here amongst your friends, that King William has now postponed his sailing? Postponed it indefinitely, although it is something urgently necessary to his interests."

She laughed at this with undisguised scorn, and looked at him almost with compassion. "I accounted you brave," she said reproachfully.

"Do you know the difference, ma'am between courage and rashness?"

But she let her thought pursue its course. "I accounted you so brave. And you start at every shadow. You conjure ghosts out of your fears. As I've said before, there may have been a dozen reasons for postponement."

"Or there may have been just one: the one you will not admit. You did not remark, I suppose, an odd coincidence; that the postponement followed closely upon its being divulged here at your house, that King William's going over to the Hague would be the occasion for the attempt?"

"Oh yes. You always feared that. But if you are right, if we are betrayed, how do we come to be still at large? Can you explain that?"

"I can. Because Bentinck still lacked the information that would enable him to lay hands upon your brother. Now, this precious piece of information, so needlessly divulged, may be in his possession to-morrow if one of us is faithless."

"Aye! If! But reassure yourself."

"By what? It is my settled view that the game is up; the risk too great to be continued." And having shed now the last vestige of his imperturbability, he fell to pleading passionately with her to disband her associates and make her escape while it was yet time. "When last I urged it, the danger, believe me, was nothing to what it has now become."

Her face grew white as she listened, her eyes almost fierce. "Yet you urged it passionately then. And nothing followed. Oh! This is a coward's counsel."

"It may be." He strove to recover his calm. "It may be. But any other leads to martyrdom. I suppose I have a vulgar mind. The prospect of martyrdom does not exalt me."

She stared at him, her bosom heaving.

"I accounted you brave," she said again, on that same deeply reproachful note. "You are the last living man from whom I should have expected this."

"Because you know that I love you."

The sheer abruptness of that declaration at such a moment, in the midst of an altercation, robbed her of breath, of colour, and of speech.

He swept on.

"Because you think that a lover must express himself in terms of knight-errantry, must talk and posture like a character in a romance, making in his exaltation a mock of life and death. Well, my lady, I am not such a lover. I have a vulgar mind, as I have said. A practical mind. I blow no iridescent bubbles to fascinate the eye and to be shivered against the first solid fact they touch. I am real, my dear; real man and real lover."

His hand sought hers; and in her half-palsied state, her senses dazed by the torrent of his oddly couched avowal, she made no attempt to deny him. He leaned over her from his fine height.

"Will you trust me, Ailsa? Will you be guided by me?"

She swayed towards him, as if drawn by some magnetic force within him. His arm went round her shoulders. Deeply stirred, an unusual excitement trembling in his voice, he added yet another question; "Will you come away with me? At once?"

That broke the spell he was weaving about her senses. "You are resolved, then, to go?"

"Only if you come with me."

She drew her hand from his clasp, her self from his lightly encircling arm. "You are mad to think it," she said, in a low, sad voice.

"Not unless I am also mad to think that you love me."

"Ian waits at Calais. Have you forgot?" It was as if she had not heard him.

"It is in my intentions that we go to him. It may be the best way to serve him now."

"And he would thank us for that service?" She shook her head, a bitter little smile on her sensitive lips. "If you know Ian at all, you know what he would say; and I know how right he would be to say it. No, no. Depart if your heart fails you. I remain with those who trust me, and for him who trusts me."

He looked at her with gloomy eyes for a long moment, reading the resolve that made her white face so stern. Then he sighed, and on that sigh the clouds lifted from his brow, and a faint smile broke from his lips. They were signs of relief, she thought, to her infinite surprise.

"Be it so," he said. "Perhaps it is better thus. For your sake, and out of my fears for you I was prepared to decamp, and so neglect what is scarcely less than a duty. But since you will not yield, it follows that I must stay for what remains to be accomplished."

They parted without further word of love between them, and Colonel Walton, leaving her bewildered and confused, went home to his lodging in Covent Garden.

To the sleek valet whom he found dutifully awaiting him, his first words brought hope.

"Dubois is still at Blackwall with the cutter?"

Lavernis' countenance brightened. "But, of course, my Colonel. We depart then? We go to France?"

"You do," said the Colonel dryly. "Be ready to set out in half an hour."

Chapter 20

Betrayal

Five days later, on the following Sunday, the 8th of June, the plotters were again assembled in the library at Lochmore House, and more than ever disposed, in view of their continued immunity from arrest, to be scornful of Colonel Walton and his prognostications of a thunderbolt which had failed to fall.

In that dark-panelled and book-lined room, whose windows looked out over the garden and the river beyond it, they waited for Mr Hay, at whose urgent request they had hurriedly been brought together.

He arrived at last. He came in with the abrupt violence of a breaking hurricane. He was out of breath, very pale, and rather wild of eye. Having made his gusty entrance, he paused on the threshold, glaring at the company.

"We are all present, I see," he said at last. "That, at least, is something."

On that he swung about, slammed the door, turned the key in the lock, withdrew it, swung about again, and struck an attitude.

"Who laughed?" he demanded fiercely.

"Faith, I did," said Colonel Walton, who sat with his back to the light beside Lady Lochmore, at the head of the long table of dark oak.

"And at what, if you please?"

"From pure relish. I delight in the grand manner, the broad gesture."

Someone else laughed with him now. Richard Hay grew pale with anger.

"Sirs, it is not the time for buffoonery, and I have little hope of being able to continue to amuse you." Dramatically, with an arm outflung, he cast his news at them.

"There is a spy amongst us. Someone here is a spy."

"Fiddlesticks!" said O'Grady, with a cackling laugh of contempt.

But he laughed alone. The assertion was too grave even for sarcasm.

"Damn your play-acting, Hay." The exclamation came from the matter-of-fact Howard. "Such a thing is unimaginable."

"As unimaginable as you please. But, nevertheless, true. So true that no one leaves the room until this spy is discovered."

"Damme!" swore Dalkeith. "You take a deal upon yourself, Mr Hay."

Stuart of Meorach turned irritably upon the speaker. He was a shrewd, practical man. "He's in the right of it, by God! If he has evidence of what he says."

"Aye! If he has evidence," sneered the sinister O'Grady.

Mr Hay snorted. "Oh, all the evidence you'll need, sirs."

Glenleven, who had sat very still and watchful of the company, stirred now impatiently. "Well, well! What is this evidence?"

"This," said Mr Hay. "Two nights ago the Auberge du Soleil at Calais was raided by a party of six English bullies, who demanded the person of Mr Richard Jerningham… "

He was interrupted there by an outcry of alarm from Lady Lochmore. The announcement had brought her suddenly to her feet.

"No, no, madam," Mr Hay made haste to reassure her. "They did not find him. By incredible luck, he had gone. By a miracle, as it seems to me – for I see no explanation for it – he had left Calais six hours before."

Still trembling she sank down again into her chair, and sat tensely attentive.

Mr Hay resumed, his manner one of suppressed fury.

"But that they sought him is enough. No one in England knew that he was there, or by what name he called himself, save only you seven and her ladyship, to whom I made it known a week ago."

Colonel Walton made an interpolation. "You may judge now, sirs, and you, my lady, whether you were justified of your resentment when I condemned that communication as unnecessary and unwise."

Glenleven brushed the interpolation aside. There was a sudden feverishness in his manner. "Yes, yes. But what's that to the matter now. Your tale, Hay? What is your tale? What do you know of these men? These bullies?"

"What I've told you. Isn't that enough? Do their damned names matter? They were English; they landed at Calais from an English ship – a swift cutter, I am informed, that waited to take them off again."

"That'll be conclusive," said Sir Hamish in the tone of one who is about to engage. He looked round, as if seeking for someone upon whom to fasten his challenge.

Her ladyship, however, was less easily satisfied.

"Whence is your information, Mr Hay?"

"Two hours ago I received a message from a friend whom I left to watch in Calais, to act as a messenger in case of need. In the present circumstances," he added with elaborate scorn, "ye'll not account it odd in me to withhold his name."

He advanced, at last, from his station by the door, his dark eyes raking the company from under the thundercloud on his brow. "Our necks, gentlemen, are not safe until we find this spy."

"Will they be safe then?" wondered the Colonel.

"Maybe not," snapped Hay. "Most probably we are already betrayed and doomed."

Little Howard sighed audibly. "Indeed, he who could tell the government so much, would be likely to tell enough to hang us all."

Colonel Walton looked wistfully into her ladyship's sad eyes. "You see," he said softly.

Glenleven, overhearing the two words, suddenly reared his head. "See what, sir? To what do you allude?"

"To my warning of this to her ladyship on Tuesday last."

Glenleven leaned forward, his face grey, his eyes gleaming with a stern malevolence. "Ah, yes," he said. "To be sure!" Then, with singular slow emphasis, he asked: "What was the knowledge that made you a prophet, sir?"

His tone, so heavily laden with suspicion that already it sounded like an accusation, startled her ladyship into intervening. "What are you implying, Jamie?"

"Colonel Walton understands me, I think. Let him answer my question."

The Colonel was not the only one who understood. He found all eyes suddenly and darkly upon him. He shrugged, indifferent. "I gave her ladyship at the time my reasons for the assumption. They were much as I had given earlier to you all. I pointed to the indiscretions that must sooner or later betray this foolery."

That brought Glenleven to his feet in anger, whilst Sir Hamish roared out: "Is foolery the best you can call this sacred enterprise of ours?"

"What I call it I told you when first I came amongst you. I call it murder. The foolery lies in the manner in which you go about it."

Mr Hay's impatience created a momentary diversion. "You talk and talk," he protested. "But nothing to the point."

"Aye. That's usual here," said Colonel Walton.

"Something to the point, I think," was Glenleven's dark reply, which ignored the sarcasm. He looked about him significantly, a plain invitation in his glance. "Need we seek further for our spy?"

There was a pause. The company sat aghast until her ladyship rose again, one hand on the chair-back to steady her, the other mechanically repressing the tumult of her bosom.

"Where do you find him, Jamie?"

"Where I should have sought him sooner had I obeyed my instincts. Oh, I own my simplicity, my guilt. Partly he fooled me by his pretence of generosity, and partly I fooled myself by my reluctance to admit that I had brought a traitor amongst us."

"Does the malice you bear him make you mad, Jamie?" she asked, her glance going to the arm he still carried in a sling.

A smile of disdain crossed his pallid face. "It is natural that you should have faith in your lover."

"My lover!" She threw up her head sharply, defiant of the general stir.

"Do you deny what we have all perceived? That he is your lover? That he has made love to you?"

She had no thought of denying it. "And that proves him a spy?" Her scorn was withering. "You reason nobly, Jamie."

"No. Not nobly. Shrewdly. Because he is your lover, he warns you, as he says: he seeks to abstract you from an enterprise which he knows is doomed. Does not that convict him? Whence came his knowledge?"

"Whence?" She paused, at a loss, suddenly stricken by the terrible logic of Glenleven's reasoning. She turned to Colonel Walton, who sat there so quietly, the only one who retained his calm, the ghost of a smile even hovering upon his lips.

"Answer him. Oh answer him!"

He knew from the blend of pain and fear in her voice that she was asking him not only to answer his accuser, but to answer the sudden, dreadful doubt the accusation had sown in her own mind.

"Was the knowledge so far to seek?" he asked. "Would not the simplest reasoning discover it? I knew the thing was doomed because I knew that which you have only just discovered: that there is a betrayer amongst us."

"And, by God," cried Dalkeith, "you had cause to know it."

171

"Here's brazen impudence," thundered Sir Hamish in fury.

And then Mr Hay, almost sinister, despite his fripperies, and very grim of tone, intervened curtly. "It is enough for me. The garden, I think." He tapped his sword-hilt significantly. "Let the honour be mine."

Glenleven shook his head, and with his sound hand caught Mr Hay by the arm. He had experience of the Colonel's skill. "We'll have no sword-play. We give no chances to spies. But the garden certainly."

Lord Claybourne, however, checked the beginnings of a general movement of aggression towards the Colonel. "Sirs, sirs! Let us consider well what we do." His normal urbanity was almost turned to dolefulness.

"What's left to consider?" wondered the stormy Dalkeith.

And but for the cool intrepidity of the Colonel's bearing, which acted as a more potent check upon them than the intervention of Lord Claybourne, it is probable that the attack would not have been stayed. He had made no shift even to rise. He sat back in his chair, without so much as troubling to uncross his legs, and the disdain in his glance, and in his tone now as he spoke, were as a rampart about his person.

"You are consistent, sirs, at least in your rashness. What's to consider, asks Harry Dalkeith. You might consider, for instance, whether some form of trial should not precede execution. Or is it that you are so in love with assassination that you must recklessly be practising it on every opportunity?"

He paused there, unabashed under the angry eyes of those men, whose impetuosity he curbed, momentarily, at least, by his cold contemptuous questions. He turned now more particularly to Glenleven.

"You build a specious accusation, sir, upon hollow suspicion, ill-digested assumption, and blundering inferences, which could carry conviction to none but a pack of fools turned craven by the fear of discovery."

They growled at him for this. But he went on undeterred.

"Ask yourselves before it is too late whether this light and easy assumption of my guilt may not, indeed, consummate your ruin, by leaving the real traitor amongst you undiscovered."

That made a perceptible impression. It left them hesitating, looking at one another now with such doubt in their glances as to show the Colonel how fully he had been understood; how in asking them, for their own sakes, to review their conviction of his guilt, he had made each man suspicious of his neighbour.

And then Claybourne, who so far had said little, and whose voice carried weight, having, in their view, royal authority behind it, expressed the doubt that had suddenly been planted in the minds of all.

"It is possible that we are being hasty. After all, appearances can be deceptive. It is possible – just possible – that, as Colonel Walton says, by too lightly fastening the guilt upon him, we may allow the real culprit to escape."

As if accepting the hint in Lord Claybourne's words, Dalkeith assumed a forensic manner.

"You have said, Colonel Walton, that you knew five days ago that there was a spy amongst us."

"I should perhaps have said that I suspected it," the Colonel corrected himself.

"You had grounds for that suspicion?"

"Is it usual to suspect without grounds?"

"What were your grounds?" came sharply from Glenleven.

The Colonel did not immediately answer. He appeared to be considering and his grey eyes played over the company before him like points of steel.

"I should prefer to withhold them yet awhile," he said, at last. "I am still too much in the position of an accused to turn accuser."

"A poor subterfuge," said Sir Hamish.

The Colonel pondered him gravely. "Oh, yes, admittedly a subterfuge. But not quite the kind you deem it."

"On my soul," cried the impetuous Mr Hay from the foot of the table, "you'll let the fellow talk you out of your wits."

"Och, now, and hasn't he done it already?" cried O'Grady. "Ye're easily bubbled, gentlemen, if you let such balderdash impose upon you."

"And so far, you will observe," Glenleven coldly pointed out, "nothing that he has said denies the accusation."

This brought again an impatient almost an anguished remonstrance from her ladyship. "Oh, why don't you give them the plain lie, Colonel Walton?"

"Have patience," he begged her. "Patience and a little faith."

"The patience will come easier than the faith," sneered Glenleven. "Come, sir! You trifle with us."

The exclamation must have found a ready echo in those rash minds, for now the storm that had momentarily been stayed, broke forth again, led by the histrionic Mr Hay.

"To the garden with him! Let us have done."

Stuart of Meorach, his gooseberry eyes protruding beyond their wont on his plump face, laid a hand upon his hilt. "You're entirely right, Hay. There has been enough of this. Too much, indeed. Outside, sir, if you please."

Howard added something to the same effect, whilst young Dalkeith strode across to fling open the French windows; and they might have swept matters there and then to a conclusion, despite her ladyship's almost frantic attempt to restrain them, if it had not still been for the dominating calm of the Colonel's own demeanour.

He rose without haste or visible perturbation.

"Give me a little moment yet before you murder me," he requested, so courteously that he seemed to mock them. "There is still something I can tell you that may completely change your opinion of me. Hear me an instant."

He dominated them by that incredible composure, almost formidable in the face of such a situation.

"Be brief, then," Sir Hamish admonished him. "Our patience is at an end."

"It shall not be tried much further. Mr Hay spoke of the incredible luck of Ian Macdonald in having been away from Calais at the time of the raid. He described it as a miracle, I think. If I could show you, prove to you, that this miracle was of my contriving, would you account it evidence that I am no traitor?"

Upon the utter silence of amazement following this question beat her ladyship's voice, strained and incredulous. And incredulous, too, was her frowning glance.

"You contrived it? You?"

And from Glenleven came another question, incisively pertinent. "How did you contrive it?"

"I sent word to Invernaion that an attempt would be made to seize him."

"You sent him word?" cried her ladyship, her voice slow with unbelief. And again there was Glenleven, his white face distorted by anger, savagely following up her question. "Why should you have sent him word? How did you know, how could you know that this attempt would be made?"

Dalkeith laughed scornfully, and O'Grady, grim and sardonic, interjected: "Aye! Answer that, now."

"Haven't I told you that I had concluded there was a spy amongst you? And wouldn't his object here, next to the discovery of the plot itself, be to discover and betray the whereabouts of Invernaion?"

Claybourne took up the questioning. "You say you sent him word." This time, however, his usual suavity failed him. He spoke in the harshly contemptuous tone of one who for the sake of form pursues a trail that he knows to be false. "How did you send it?"

"By my servant Lavernis. I dispatched him to Calais on Tuesday night, as soon as I had left here, after hearing Mr Hay's message. Lavernis arrived in Calais twenty-four hours ahead of the government agents. He carried a letter from me which contained the warning that sent Invernaion on his travels. By my instructions Lavernis stayed to see what might happen. He witnessed the raid on the Auberge du Soleil by Monsieur Bentinck's men – there were six of them, landed from an English vessel, as Mr Hay has told you – and he arrived back here last night."

"That was prompt travelling." Claybourne spoke in the same tone of scornful unbelief. "How did he come to accomplish it? By what resources?"

"I have a cutter at my orders, a little way down the river, with a mixed crew, most of them smugglers ordinarily, but at present in my pay."

It seemed to them all then that he was recklessly piling falsehood upon falsehood in the desperate hope of duping them. But of all the incredible things he had told them in the last few minutes, this tale of a ship and crew in his pay was quite the most incredible.

They stood in gaping silence under those cold eyes of his, which shifted from face to face in constant, watchful scrutiny. That Colonel Walton, in the circumstances to which it was known that gaming had reduced him, should assert that he kept a cutter at his charges was fantastic. It was to push mendacity beyond all plausible limits.

"By God!" said O'Grady in sheer wonder, "if ye suppose we'll be swallowing that, then, saving her ladyship's presence, ye're as big a fool as Muldoon's calf, that ran a mile to suck a bull."

"That expresses it," Glenleven agreed. "The knave is lying. Lying impudently."

The Colonel's glance, passing over the Major, came to settle upon his lordship.

"Knave, eh?" he said. "Knave and liar. We'll leave the knave for the moment. But as for the liar, it happens that I have evidence under my hand to prove my words."

Chapter 21

The Trap

Under the wondering eyes of the company Colonel Walton ripped away the bullion which edged his baldrick and served to hold together the two strips of fine leather that composed it. As these now gaped apart, he took from between them a folded sheet of paper. This paper he unfolded, and then paused, considering the faces before him, like a man who is making choice.

At last, speaking slowly, "Whoever here is dishonest," he said, "it cannot, I think, be you, Lord Claybourne."

"I am obliged to you, sir, for the compliment," said his lordship, not without suspicion of sarcasm.

"Also you hold in this company a position which gives you the right to my preference." He leaned forward, and proffered the unfolded sheet. "This should help you, my lord, to attach faith to my word."

Frowning his perplexity, Claybourne advanced a step, and took the paper slowly. Glenleven and Dalkeith moved forward also, to scan it with him, but suddenly found a barrier in Walton's outstretched arm.

"For the moment, if you please, it is for Lord Claybourne's eyes alone." The Colonel's tone was peremptory.

Dalkeith shrugged.

"Why this?" asked her ladyship. And Glenleven, his eyes hard, looked as if he would use insistence, when a sudden exclamation from Lord Claybourne drew the attention of them all.

His lordship held the sheet in a hand that had begun to tremble, and there was a deep frown of perplexity between eyes that in their intentness seemed to bulge as they read. He walked away towards the window, as if to scan the writing in the stronger light. When, presently, he turned again, his face was blank with amazement, almost with awe; and he addressed Colonel Walton on a note that was entirely new, a note unmistakably of deference.

"But why, sir, did you not... "

Colonel Walton interrupted him. And into his voice, too, a change had come. It was invested now with a clear tone of authority.

"No more on that at the moment, sir." Quietly but with a firm assurance, he recovered the paper from his lordship's hands, folded it, put it into his pocket.

"If you are now, my lord, as I hope you are, persuaded that what I have said is true, and that whoever is the spy – and a spy is certainly present – I am not likely to be the man, perhaps you will give the company that assurance, so that no more precious time may be wasted."

"I do so. Unhesitatingly." His lordship was emphatic. "I will beg you, sirs, to take my word for that." His manner suggested that he flung down a gage of battle to any man who still questioned Colonel Walton's probity.

Glenleven was the only one who declined to be impressed. He stood scowling, irritated by the exclusion from this secret of a person so important as himself.

"What's this?" he demanded. "Where is the need for mystery? If that paper is evidence of anything, isn't it evidence for us all?"

Colonel Walton considered him with an exasperating calm.

"Why so it shall be. Presently. First, however, I have other evidence for you, free to you all; that of my servant Lavernis. I have brought him with me. He waits here, in the servants' hall, to give you his own account of his voyage to Calais, and to be questioned by you, so that you may test the truth of what he tells you, and of what I have told you."

Her ladyship intervened. "But is so much still necessary, since my Lord Claybourne... "

"Most necessary," snapped Glenleven with a discourtesy that set them staring. "I take no man's word, no man's judgment of evidence that I have not examined for myself." It was plain from his glance and gesture that he alluded to the paper Claybourne had scrutinized. It was plain also how deeply anger moved him. The hand he had flung out was seen to shake.

Colonel Walton observing him closely, if with apparent languor, smiled faintly upon this white heat.

"I cannot blame you, my lord, for practising, in some respects at least, the virtue of prudence. But you shall be satisfied. Rest assured of that. Fully satisfied." He turned to the company generally. "When you shall have questioned my servant and heard his answers, you will have learnt all that you could desire to know." He made a slight pause, and then added: "Not only will the particular treachery that has been practised here be clear to you beyond all doubt, but you should be assisted in the discovery of the identity of our betrayer – of the man who must not be suffered to leave this house alive. It has been said, I think, that there is no Prendergass here. And that, at least remains true, unless I am greatly at fault. Prendergass was an honest man who betrayed from motives of conscience. Our betrayer will be found, I believe, to be just a Judas who sells his master. At least, that is my surmise. But you should be able to form your own conclusions after you have questioned Lavernis." He paused there again, and his eyes, hard and stern, passed slowly from one to another of those startled faces. Then he resumed his seat.

"Let someone fetch my servant."

Glenleven was the only one who offered to run that errand; and he offered promptly.

"I'll go, myself," he announced, and on the words was turning towards the door. In his haste he almost stumbled. It was an unnecessary haste, for, as the Colonel observed, none of the others sought to dispute with him the office he assumed.

Finding the door locked, he turned impatiently. "The key, Mr Hay."

He held out a hand that still trembled visibly from the fury shaking him.

Hay, who, like the others, had been reduced to limp bewilderment, fumbled a moment in his pocket for the key, produced it, and surrendered it. Irritably Glenleven snatched it from him. Using his left hand, he blundered with it a moment at the lock; then, having succeeded in turning it, was gone, slamming the door after him.

"So!" said the Colonel, and laughed very softly. "So!"

He was instantly to his feet and moving swiftly down the room to the French windows that opened upon the garden. He flung them wide; then he turned again, and spoke with brisk authority.

"Sirs, if you are to assure the safety of your necks, I have a shrewd notion that your presence is very urgently required in the courtyard. It is life or death for you, gentlemen. I beg that you will follow me." And he added more lightly, "I think that I shall have something interesting to show you."

Claybourne in promptest obedience was at his side almost before he had finished speaking. Thence, to confirm him, his lordship flung a sharp word of command over his shoulder that brought the pack after him in blind alacrity.

To her ladyship's startled eyes they seemed to tumble from the room in their precipitancy.

She followed to the window; but no farther. Thence she saw them racing at the Colonel's heels along the flank of the house, to vanish round the angle of its façade.

They were no more than in time to behold what Colonel Walton counted upon finding there.

As they swung into the flagged courtyard before the mansion, they had a view of my Lord Glenleven, hatless, taking the six steps from the door at a single, perilous leap, and racing for the gateway.

Whatever may have been the first thoughts of those gentlemen at sight of this portent, to O'Grady it seems to have presented no riddle. This at least is the conclusion to be drawn from the view-holloa he loosed after an instant's gasping pause.

"Tally-ho!" He charged forward furiously at the Colonel's heels. "Yoicks! Yoicks! Tally-ho!"

Had not the tall wrought-iron gates been closed, Glenleven must have gained the Strand before they could reach him, and things might have been more difficult. As it was, whilst his left hand fumbled clumsily with the latch, the Colonel was upon him, pulling him back, so that the others might surround him.

Wayfarers in the Strand paused to peer through the railings, wondering what novel madcap game was this that was being played in the courtyard of Lochmore House by gentlemen in laced coats and periwigs.

"It's meat for hounds ye are, ye mangy fox!" O'Grady saluted the Viscount with his ugly laugh.

"Whither away in such haste, Glenleven?" was Stuart's fierce demand, his powerful hand on the captive's shoulder.

Colonel Walton, squarely before him, was smiling grimly into his lordship's eyes. "Faith, I'm much obliged to you, my lord. Will you come back with us?"

"And explain yourself?" Claybourne added sternly.

There was a snarl of despair on Glenleven's grey face; his eyes glared like those of a trapped beast into the incredulously angry countenances about him. Instinct drove him to attempt to draw his sword with his left hand. But the press about him was too close to give him elbowroom; and whilst he struggled someone deprived him of sword and sword-belt.

It may have been in his mind to call to those inquisitive passers-by in the Strand for assistance, to raise a cry of treason and murder that might bring a rescue. But the Colonel was too prompt and expert. Glenleven's periwig was pulled over his face to blind and half-choke him. Lifted helplessly off his feet he was borne swiftly up the steps, across the hall, down a corridor to the rear of the house, and so back into the room he had so lately quitted, where her bewildered ladyship waited.

Seeing him brought in forcibly, and in such disarray, she cried out to know the reason.

Colonel Walton explained to her that which already had explained itself to all those who had shared the swift brief hunt with him.

"It's just that his lordship must have misunderstood me. He can't have heard me say that Lavernis was in the servants' hall, or else he knew that I was lying when I said it, as, indeed, I was. That was a little trap I set. It occurred to me that our traitor, perceiving that the game was lost, would disclose himself by his eagerness to respond to my request that someone should fetch my servant. It would supply him with the pretext he so urgently needed to escape from a house that had suddenly become very dangerous to him.

"My Lord Glenleven, ma'am, had no thought for my servant. We only just caught him at the gate, going in such haste that he had not even stayed to get his hat."

She understood, as those had understood who had witnessed that self-betraying flight, and understanding she stood there, a pale incarnation of conflicting horror and unbelief. When at last she could find words, it was only to express the unbelief which had conquered horror. "Oh, but this is mad! Impossible! Impossible!"

"Merely incredible," said the Colonel, and as she looked at the set faces of the other five, she saw that every man of them shared the Colonel's conviction.

Nor was there in Glenleven's aspect anything to contradict them. They had pulled the blond wig from his face, and thrust him into a chair, where he sat now, limp and panting, his face mottled, terror in his eyes, disorder in his clothes from the rough handling he had received.

The young Countess drew a step nearer to him. "Jamie! What does it mean?" There was anguish in her voice.

The instinct to bluster asserted itself in him. "Do I know what it means? Best ask these fools. Best warn them, too, to have a care how far they carry their damned idiocy."

Major O'Grady standing over him laughed grimly at the threat. Sir Hamish on the other side heaped contumely upon him.

"You villain! You damned, smooth, slimy villain! And you a Macdonald!"

This inspired O'Grady to emulation. His nut-cracker face inflamed, he leaned over, shaking a fist within an inch of his lordship's nose.

"Ye foul spawn of Iscariot! I can scarce believe it even now, ye white-faced omadhaun. I'd as soon have believed it of myself, so I would."

"It's just incredible, stab me!" said the willowy Dalkeith, and sighed dejectedly.

And then Glenleven roused himself to a fiercer passion. "If it's incredible, you numskulls, why do you credit it? Don't you see that this rogue… "

Claybourne interrupted him sternly. "Tell us whither you were going in such hot haste. If you don't want us to believe you a villain, tell us that."

"I'll tell you something else that is to the point. This man here, this rogue who is leading you all by the nose, so as to avert suspicion from himself, has been petitioning Lord Portland for employment ever since he came to England, over a year ago, and to my certain knowledge Portland has given him employment. Employment to come here and spy upon us and betray us. There's our betrayer. There's Portland's spy. There! Ask him. Let him deny that, if he can. You ask me where I went. I went to fetch you the proof of that before it was too late."

"Again I am much obliged to your lordship," said the Colonel quietly. "You make things clear and easy." He looked round with the utmost composure. "It is quite true that he says: that I am so employed by Monsieur Bentinck. I will explain that presently. Meanwhile, let him now tell you how he knows it."

"How I know it?" screamed Glenleven. "I know it… " He caught his breath. "I know it," he ended doggedly.

"So much is plain, since you stated it. What I am asking you is how you know it," the Colonel insisted, his glittering eye upon the Viscount's white, tortured face.

"My God! Am I to be questioned by you? By a spy! You've all heard him admit it. Because he knows it would be futile to deny it. You've heard him admit it. That he is Bentinck's jackal. And you do nothing!"

Claybourne interposed his large figure. "Enough of this ranting, Glenleven. Whither were you going in such haste? Answer that."

"I've answered it. Be damned to you!"

But Claybourne insisted.

"You said something of fetching proofs. What proofs, Glenleven?"

The trapped man glared impotent fury and impotent fear. Invention failed him. Again bluster was his only resource.

"I deny your right to question me. I am not on my trial. You may assume what you please, you fools. You fools!"

Lady Lochmore advanced again until she came to stand immediately before him.

"Will you tell me, Jamie, why you did this?" she asked him in a voice of ice. "Why should you, of all men, have been our betrayer?"

In the silence that was held for him he just scowled at her without answering. At last his eyes fell away, under her clear, stern gaze.

"Lord in Heaven!" she cried. "Have you nothing to say? Nothing? Ian saved your life. At his own great peril, with a price upon his head, he came here to London to rescue you. It cannot have been his ruin that you sought. Was it mine, Jamie? Was this your revenge on me?"

She questioned him on something she could understand and even perhaps forgive. So much was to be read in her tone, which suddenly had become almost pleading. But he sat there sullenly silent now, a figure half-tragic, half-ridiculous, with his periwig awry above his white, narrow face.

Colonel Walton undertook to answer for him. At her ladyship's elbow, he spoke quietly.

"He did it, I think, for the same reason that he conceived this plot against the life of William of Orange. So that he might entrap your brother and deliver him to a government that has placed a price upon his head."

"That's a foul invention," cried Glenleven, and would have risen, but that O'Grady and Stuart between them forced him down again into his chair.

Lady Lochmore paid no heed to his denial. She had swung round to stare at Colonel Walton, a wildness in her dark blue eyes, an anguish disordering her white beauty.

Her voice choked a little as she challenged him.

"Colonel Walton, who are you? What are you? What is your part in this?"

The Colonel bowed his head. "I think it is time I told you," he said.

Chapter 22

The Accredited Agent

At Colonel Walton's request, all were seated save O'Grady and Sir Hamish Stuart, who remained on guard over the limp, huddled figure of Glenleven. Her ladyship had gone back to her chair at the head of the table, and she sat there, stiff and straight, her white hands gripping the arms of it. The others had disposed themselves about one side of it so as to face the Colonel, who from the hearth commanded the assembly.

A sustained and absolute calm of manner can in itself be negatively and very effectively offensive, by the utter lack of deference which it implies. This, as you know, had been the demeanour that had marked the Colonel in his dealings with these plotters in the past. Now it was subtly changed. And the change was for the worse.

As he stood there, tall and commanding, his aspect was stern to the point of being forbidding.

"First," he said, "my Lord Claybourne shall answer your ladyship's question as to what I am."

Claybourne, inclining his head as if in acknowledgment of a command, was prompt to obey. "Colonel Walton," he said, "is the accredited agent of King James to his loyal subjects in England. The paper which you saw him show me is a letter to him in His Majesty's own hand. It is virtually Colonel Walton's commission to represent His Majesty here, and it exhorts all those who are still His

186

Majesty's loyal subjects and whose assistance Colonel Walton may require on His Majesty's behalf, to render it as they would render it to the King himself."

He ceased. Round eyes of men whose very breathing seemed suspended in astonishment, stared at him, and from him, almost in awe, to the impassive Colonel, whom an hour ago they had clamoured to put to death as a spy.

Dudley Walton came forward, drew the letter from his pocket, and laid it on the table.

"You will all understand now why this could not be disclosed until I had sprung my little trap to catch the traitor. The letter is there for your inspection."

Whilst they conned it with respect and interest, he returned to the hearth, and once more put his shoulders to the overmantel.

"That accounts for me, but not entirely. I owe this commission partly to the confidence His Majesty does me the honour to repose in me; but quite as much to the fact that at a time when His Majesty urgently required an agent here to investigate the feeling of the country, I very opportunely inherited a small estate in Wiltshire.

"You may or you may not know, sirs, that Monsieur Bentinck is so well served by spies at Saint Germains that every arrival and departure there is promptly reported here. In my own case, my Wiltshire inheritance supplied a plausible reason for my return to England; and the natural desire to enjoy the inheritance supplied a no less plausible reason for an anxiety on my part to make my peace with King William's government. To make quite sure that no suspicion should attach to me, I departed from Saint Germains universally despised as a venal deserter of the cause. This would not fail to be reported to Bentinck.

"To consolidate my position I offered, immediately on arrival, my services to the existing government, well knowing that they would not be accepted. That was not the only fraud I practised. That I speedily broke myself at play was another pretence, necessary so as to explain the early sale of my little heritage and my subsequent wanderings.

"On my return to London, six weeks ago, I renewed my offer of services to King William, so as to provide myself, in the certain event of refusal, with such a pretext for departure from England as should leave no obstacle to my coming back again if it became necessary.

"I shall return to this.

"The presence of an agent here at the time, to make the tour of England which I made, was rendered necessary by the failure of the enterprise which has come to be known as the Assassination Plot, but in the assassination part of which, I, for one, am not to be persuaded that His Majesty had any hand or wish.

"To shelter themselves from the consternation and horror following upon the discovery of that plot, all Jacobites had gone to ground. It was become impossible to compute how many of these could be depended upon to come forth again when and if King Louis should send over an army. My task was the difficult one of investigating this at close quarters. Hence all the elaborate precautions which I took.

"I will say only that the hopes in which I came found no smallest encouragement. Loyalty I discovered in plenty; but the courage to express it, to stake all upon a throw, in short, to take up arms against the usurper is, as I told you when first I came amongst you, everywhere absent at this present time, utterly stifled by the discovery of the plot of two years ago. Later on I do not doubt that this courage will revive; especially if the present government should give rise to discontent, and provided that in the meantime there are no more assassination plots to discredit King James and arouse even Tory sympathy for King William."

He paused again, to allow those last, sternly-spoken words to sink into the hearts of his audience.

"My task here was done. I was on the point of returning to France to make my disheartening report to His Majesty when Lord Glenleven informed me of the existence of this plot of yours, and invited me to join it."

His delivery became now more slow and distinct than ever.

"If I had done my duty, I should at once have disclosed my commission to Glenleven and used my authority under it to exact from him the nature and details of the plot. Upon learning these – and in spite of whatever may meanwhile have taken place in France, or of whatever authority Invernaion may conceive that he possesses – I must have commanded the immediate abandonment of this undertaking, as being inopportune and likely at this present time lastingly to injure His Majesty's cause. That was my clear duty.

"For reasons which I do not propose to state, I temporized. I was considering how to act in such a way as to serve not only His Majesty's interests, but also certain sudden interests of my own. Whilst I was so considering, the unexpected happened. It was then that so as to account for my lingering in England and so as to provide for my probable return, I had again communicated with Monsieur Bentinck. To my surprise, Bentinck sent for me. Believing me as hard driven by circumstances as I had represented, that impudent Dutchman had the effrontery to offer me employment as a spy.

"He showed himself acquainted with the fact that I had received from Glenleven an invitation to join your conspiracy, and his instructions to me were that I should accept the invitation. I was to join you so that I might discover for him the only two facts of which Monsieur Bentinck appeared to be still in ignorance: the occasion when the attack on the Prince of Orange was to be made and the whereabouts of the elusive and dangerous Ian Macdonald of Invernaion, so that his troublesome person might be seized by Bentinck's agents.

"In my indignation at the insult of such an offer, and at whatever ultimate cost to myself, I was about to return the only answer which it demanded when I was checked by the perception of what you must be perceiving: something very odd, very mysterious in the proposal.

"Monsieur Bentinck had used an almost excessive frankness: not only did he reveal himself fully aware of the nature and aim of this plot of yours, not only did he assert that he knew the names of all engaged in it, but he knew also – as I have already said – that Lord Glenleven had already invited me to join it.

"At first I took this for pure assumption. But when I came to consider further, to add it to the rest of his knowledge, I began to persuade myself that there must be already a spy amongst you. But if this were so, why should Bentinck employ me to ascertain that which the existing spy could ascertain so easily? And why should he be so recklessly frank in betraying to me the wide knowledge he already possessed? I might in my turn betray it to you, and thus frustrate the government's chief aim, which was to seize the person of Ian Macdonald.

"These were bewildering questions; and I could answer them only by assumptions. The first was that perhaps Bentinck did not fully trust the spy he was already employing. The second was that Bentinck's faith that I would not betray him must rest upon the conviction that I was a needy and venal scoundrel unable to resist the seduction of the high reward offered for information that would lead to Invernaion's capture. He certainly had some grounds for this. I had been known for a Jacobite, and I was petitioning King William's government for employment; that in itself did not make me respected. I proclaimed that my only fidelity was to the hand that paid me; I allowed it to appear that I was not only a broken gamester, but a man who did not scruple to trade upon his antecedents so as to exploit the generosity of Jacobites.

"Was it difficult, then, to suppose that Bentinck should be acting upon those contemptuous assumptions?

"Certain it is that if I had refused his offer, I should never have been suffered to leave the Palace. This, however, was not my reason for accepting.

"For I did accept, as Glenleven has informed you. This to his own further undoing, since he cannot tell you how he comes by that knowledge without confessing himself what I now know him to be."

Glenleven stirred convulsively. He attempted to rear himself as if to answer. But his guards repressed him, and this with a roughness which showed how little they desired interruptions at this moment.

"I accepted," the Colonel resumed, "so that I might probe this mystery, and discover and deliver you from the betrayer of whose existence I was persuaded.

"At first Bentinck's knowledge of what had passed between Glenleven and myself in the course of an early morning walk from Gascoigne's seemed – if he had not drawn a bow at a venture – to circumscribe the field of my search. Only one man knew of that besides Glenleven himself, and to suspect Glenleven then was out of the question. That man was Major O'Grady, who had been with us that night at Gascoigne's until we set out together, and who had been close in talk with Glenleven just before.

"Subsequent reflection showed me, however, that Glenleven's intention to draw me into the plot must have been known to you all, and so I sought confirmation of my assumption.

"Now it is common knowledge that there is no man so vulnerable to the corrupting influence of gold as he who is in need. I sought amongst you the man whose circumstances were most straitened, and again the path led straight to Major O'Grady. It began to seem to me that I need look no further."

"It's much obliged to you I am, on my soul!" O'Grady grumbled. "A sweet flattery."

The Colonel acknowledged the interruption by a fleeting smile, and went on.

"But whilst hunting with the hounds, I attempted also to run with the hare. It was my duty to King James to stifle this conspiracy, and my concern for Lady Lochmore urged me to remove her from it. My attempt in this direction brought a quarrel on my hands, very odd and reckless at such a time, followed by a reconciliation even more odd in its abruptness.

"I sought an explanation of that in Lord Glenleven's relations with Lady Lochmore. I confess that my first conjecture was that he had been moved to his recklessness by perceiving in me a possible rival to her ladyship's affections. But my investigations revealed that he was not only her next of kin, but, of course, Ian Macdonald's, and that he was heir to the very considerable dominion of Invernaion.

They also revealed that Glenleven's gambling father had left him a very restricted patrimony. Then I discovered that hopes entertained by Glenleven of mending his fortunes by marrying Lady Lochmore had been definitely and finally quenched by her ladyship.

"Gradually the nasty truth began to emerge. If Ian Macdonald perished, James Macdonald, Viscount Glenleven, would succeed to lands which, out of consideration for services to King William, might be spared from confiscation."

He was interrupted there by a general stir, and an outburst of incredulous anger from Dalkeith, who fiercely protested that the Colonel went too far in his conclusions.

Encouraged by this, Glenleven roused himself. "It's all lies! A mass of wicked, reckless assumptions, as you shall discover."

"It's an explanation," the Colonel amended sternly. "The only explanation that fits all the facts."

Their bewildered looks showed him how far it still was from explaining matters to them.

"You don't yet understand?" He smiled a little wearily. "Let me explain.

"Such a game as Glenleven played is fraught with peril. First there is such peril as that which has now overtaken him. Then, if successful, there is peril as great afterwards to the enjoyment of the fruits of his treachery.

"What would men have said at Invernaion when they found Glenleven lord of estates inherited from one who had perished in a treason that Glenleven had shared? Could he have escaped suspicion of being what he is? Would the clansmen have allowed him to survive that suspicion?

"To avoid this it became necessary that he should provide himself with a stalking-horse; a stalking-horse to be sacrificed when the hunt was ended and the kill was made.

"That was the condition he made with Bentinck. It is not to be supposed that it would be difficult to make. Monsieur Bentinck out of fear and love for his master William of Orange, would be prepared to agree almost to anything so that he might lay by the heels an enemy so resolute, bold, fanatical and elusive as Invernaion had proved himself to be. What, after all, to Bentinck was the lordship of some acres in the Highlands of Scotland compared with the peace of mind to be gained from the suppression of Ian Macdonald?

"Anyway, that, I concluded, was the bargain that had been made."

The admission that these were but conclusions was Glenleven's cue wildly to interrupt him.

"You concluded! You admit that all this is just what you concluded. My God! are your rash conclusions to convict a man of the things of which you accuse me? Am I to be constrained here to listen to these infamous lies? Is this your sense of justice, you cowards? Seven of you against one man! And not a proof, not a pennyworth of proof of anything he says. I made a bargain with my Lord of Portland, he glibly tells you. When did I make this bargain? When? What was the occasion?"

"I think I can tell you that," the Colonel quietly answered him. "You bring me to the very starting-point of my conclusions."

He had turned half-aside, and was addressing himself now directly to Glenleven.

"After Invernaion at the risk of his life had rescued you from the gallows by kidnapping de la Rue, he was induced to do a like heroic service for Sir John Fenwick. But the government, outraged at seeing its justice cheated in this manner, took the course of dealing with Sir John by bill of attainder. That course having been once discovered, there was no reason why it should not also have been applied to your case.

"Why, I asked myself, had this not been done? I made inquiries, and I discovered that at the time when you dreaded re-arrest, you were actually summoned by Lord Portland to Kensington Palace. What passed between you at that interview? What undertakings did Portland extract from you, that you did not go from Kensington Palace to the Tower? At what price did you obtain that no bill of attainder should be moved against you, whilst Sir John Fenwick paid with his head for a treason notoriously less black than yours?

"The answer is because it was in your power to betray, and it proved also in your nature to betray, one whose activities the government really feared. You would give the government Invernaion's life as the price of your own. To accomplish it, and so that you might draw him into a trap, you conceived and set on foot this conspiracy modelled upon the Assassination Plot. But so that your part in its subsequent betrayal should never appear, so that you might be free to enjoy the blood-wealth you were to earn, you brought me in to be your stalking-horse, and afterwards the chief witness against Invernaion at his trial." His cold, accusing glance, which had been fixed upon Glenleven, came back to the company about the table. "Now you understand why I was employed. Thus publicly disclosed at the trial as the betrayer, I made Glenleven safe from any suspicion that might disturb his enjoyment of the fruits of his treachery."

He ceased, and silence followed. Out of set, forbidding countenances eyes of loathing were turned upon Glenleven where he sat, limp and pallid, the fear of death before him. As if those condemning eyes acted upon him like so many goads, he rallied under them. He leaned forward, cunning and fury surmounting the fear in him.

"You have heard him, eh?" His lips were twisted into a leer. "You have listened to his tissue of falsehood, and you are convinced by it, you fools. Yet at a breath I can demolish it, like the cobweb that it is." His voice, usually so musical, came harsh and shrill. "If what this man says is true, if I needed him for a stalking-horse, if he was so valuable to me, so precious to me, should I have put a duel upon him and sought his life? Should I? Ask yourselves, sirs!"

Stuart of Meorach replied before Colonel Walton could do so. I have said that, for all his heat, he was a man of shrewd perceptions.

"I, for one, have asked myself that already. But the answer doesn't help you, you villain. That was an action of panic on your part when you discovered Colonel Walton making efforts to detach her ladyship and her brother from the plot. If he were to succeed in that design, your foul scheme would be ruined; your victim would escape; and your chance of fortune would be lost to you. So you chose what you conceived to be the lesser evil. Does any doubt that explanation? Isn't it plain enough?" His prominent eyes swept fiercely round the board, only to meet conviction on every countenance.

The Colonel gravely nodded. "It was his unnatural haste to be reconciled with me after he had failed in that encounter which first aroused my suspicions. He had then no alternative but to accept the risk he would have avoided, and it only remained for him to rest his hopes entirely upon prevailing in spite of me. It was in this that he overreached himself."

He paused there, thoughtfully. Then he fetched a sigh. "That, I think, is all that I can tell you of this nasty matter."

"And more than enough, as God's my life!" said Geoffrey Howard, adding with terrible significance: "We know what remains to be done."

There was the commencement of a general stir at this, and suddenly Glenleven was struggling with those who guarded him. He broke into blasphemy and protestations.

"Damn you for a pack of fools," he cried at the end of them. "You'll never endanger your silly necks by believing this string of lies."

"Och, of course not," O'Grady mocked him, a broad grin on his nut-cracker face. "Why should we when ye can so easily be dispelling them? Just tell us, now, where ye were going in such a hurry when we caught you at the gate."

Glenleven glared at him in anguish.

Colonel Walton looked wistful. "But that I scared him into that act of self-betrayal, you might indeed require more proof than I can furnish."

"Not even then," said Sir Hamish. "Let us have done."

"Ah, no, no! In mercy not…not his life!" her ladyship begged.

Mr Hay heaved himself up with an oath. "My lady, it is our lives or his. It remains to find Haceldama for this Judas."

But Colonel Walton intervened.

"Let him find it for himself, like the other Judas," he said, and so provoked an uproar of dissension. He raised his hand, to repress it. "You have yourselves to consider sirs. You will derive no security from putting Glenleven to death, because he can add nothing to the information he has already given Bentinck. The government would know upon whom to avenge him, if it desired to do so.

"But he may with advantage be trussed up, and bestowed in the cellar for the next four-and-twenty hours, so as to give you so much start in scattering to your respective homes.

"Your safety lies in the fact that King William desires no martyrs. Therefore I will venture to prophesy with some confidence that provided you depart at once, and remain absent, you are not likely to be troubled."

More solemnly he added: "And this, in His Majesty's name, is what I now command you all to do."

Chapter 23

The Soul of Dudley Walton

That command issued in the name of the King Over the Water, was accepted by those misguided gentlemen as the last word. It brought matters to a speedy conclusion.

O'Grady and Sir Hamish, assisted by Mr Hay, trussed up Glenleven with perhaps unnecessary rigour, and under a running snarl of taunts from the Irishman the while. With a blow across the mouth, he had silenced the Viscount's last fierce blasphemous protest.

Whilst they were about this unpleasant business her ladyship, who had moved away to the window, without a single word spoken, stood there with her back to the room. Only the droop of her shoulders which normally were so proudly carried, gave an indication of the dejection into which she had been plunged.

There at the window she remained after Glenleven had been carried out; and she was still in that attitude after each of those sorely disheartened conspirators had briefly and feelingly taken leave of Colonel Walton, the representative of majesty.

She did not even turn when Lord Claybourne approached her to offer her his services, to place himself at her commands. It was in a stifled voice that she thanked him and declined his aid.

"Give yourself no thought for me, my lord," she ended, and without moving she made a gesture of gentle dismissal.

197

Claybourne caught the hand she so extended, and bending from his stately height, kissed it in valediction.

The others followed, one by one, each taking the hand which she yielded without turning, and each, with a murmured word, thereafter departing.

At last, when she heard the door close and all was still, she uttered a little moan, and faced about to discover that in the room there was still another tenant beside herself.

Colonel Walton, straight, self-contained, and very elegant in his rust-red, gold-laced coat, was standing quietly at the foot of the long table.

Startled, her tear-stained eyes considered him out of a countenance upon which grief and shame had set their heavy stamp.

"Why do you stay?" she asked him, and in her voice there was an undertone that was almost fierce.

"Did you truly think I had gone? That I had left you here alone with your sorrow?" His smile was sweetly wistful.

"Why not? Why should you remain? I was of those who doubted you."

"But your doubts were justified. I did take service with Monsieur Bentinck as a spy."

"So you have stayed to mock me? Is that generous? But, to be sure, I deserve no generosity where I displayed none."

"That is why I stayed. So that you may make amends by displaying it now." He advanced upon her. He took her hands, which she surrendered without protest, almost as one in fear. "There was one thing I withheld from them: the reason why I failed in my duty when I did not disclose my commission at once to Glenleven. That is for your ear alone. Will you hear it now?"

The tone he used, rather than his words, was responsible for the sudden tumult of her breast. "That…that must be a matter for your judgment, sir."

"Ah, no. Not judgment. Judgment shall be yours. You shall pronounce it when you have heard. I neglected my duty because had

I performed it I should have been afforded, perhaps, no chance of ever seeing you again."

"You had seen me but once," she protested.

"And nothing else thereafter. As things have fallen out, it is perhaps fortunate for you all that I did neglect my duty; it is most fortunate for Invernaion; fortunate above all for the cause of King James. But is it fortunate for me?"

"For you?" And now as she looked at him wide-eyed, he perceived the dawn of a sudden alarm on her sweet, white face. The explanation of it followed: "Ah, yes. What of you? How will you escape Bentinck's anger for your breach of faith with him?"

"Oh, that!" He laughed softly, suddenly warmed by her concern. "That is far, indeed, from my preoccupations. My preparations are made. The cutter that brought Lavernis over stays for me at Blackwall. Lavernis, himself, waits here; not in your servants' hall, as I pretended, but at your water-gate there, with a boat in which to convey me straight to the cutter. For it should be plain to you that I came in the knowledge that this would be our last assembly."

"Why, then?" she said. "Then?"

"I still wait to learn if my neglect of duty, so fortunate to so many, is to be fortunate to me."

She understood him now. The tenderness of his down-slanting, melancholy eyes left nothing to be guessed.

The colour stirred in her white cheeks. She faltered a little as she asked him with instinctive feminine pretence: "What...what would make it so?"

He was blunt in his reply. "Your coming with me to France, my dear."

She faced him in sweetest frankness of surrender.

"You still wish it after my doubtings of you?"

He laughed, softly but very joyously, and boldly took her into his arms.

"It was Claybourne's opinion that you might save my soul for me. And now I am of that opinion, too."

"You impose a hard task upon me," she sighed. But the sigh was of content.

And that is how Colonel Dudley Walton returning empty-handed to Saint Germains in so far as the cause of King James was concerned, went neither empty-handed nor empty-hearted in so far as he was concerned himself.

Rafael Sabatini

Captain Blood

Captain Blood is the much-loved story of a physician and gentleman turned pirate.

Peter Blood, wrongfully accused and sentenced to death, narrowly escapes his fate and finds himself in the company of buccaneers. Embarking on his new life with remarkable skill and bravery, Blood becomes the 'Robin Hood' of the Spanish seas. This is swashbuckling adventure at its best.

The Gates of Doom

'Depend above all on Pauncefort', announced King James; 'his loyalty is dependable as steel. He is with us body and soul and to the last penny of his fortune.' So when Pauncefort does indeed face bankruptcy after the collapse of the South Sea Company, the king's supreme confidence now seems rather foolish. And as Pauncefort's thoughts turn to gambling, moneylenders and even marriage to recover his debts, will he be able to remain true to the end? And what part will his friend and confidante, Captain Gaynor, play in his destiny?

'A clever story, well and amusingly told' – *The Times*

Rafael Sabatini

The Lost King

The Lost King tells the story of Louis XVII – the French royal who officially died at the age of ten but, as legend has it, escaped to foreign lands where he lived to an old age. Sabatini breathes life into these age-old myths, creating a story of passion, revenge and betrayal. He tells of how the young child escaped to Switzerland from where he plotted his triumphant return to claim the throne of France.

'…the hypnotic spell of a novel which for sheer suspense, deserves to be ranked with Sabatini's best' – *New York Times*

Scaramouche

When a young cleric is wrongfully killed, his friend, André-Louis, vows to avenge his death. André's mission takes him to the very heart of the French Revolution where he finds the only way to survive is to assume a new identity. And so is born Scaramouche – a brave and remarkable hero of the finest order and a classic and much-loved tale in the greatest swashbuckling tradition.

'Mr Sabatini's novel of the French Revolution has all the colour and lively incident which we expect in his work' – *Observer*

Rafael Sabatini

The Sea Hawk

Sir Oliver, a typical English gentleman, is accused of murder, kidnapped off the Cornish coast, and dragged into life as a Barbary corsair. However Sir Oliver rises to the challenge and proves a worthy hero for this much-admired novel. Religious conflict, melodrama, romance and intrigue combine to create a masterly and highly successful story, perhaps best-known for its many film adaptations.

The Shame of Motley

The Court of Pesaro has a certain fool – one Lazzaro Biancomonte of Biancomonte. *The Shame of Motley* is Lazzaro's story, presented with all the vivid colour and dramatic characterisation that has become Sabatini's hallmark.

'Mr Sabatini could not be conventional or commonplace if he tried'
– *Standard*

Made in the USA
Middletown, DE
08 February 2019